IN T[

You know those names: the Pruitts, the Sinclairs, the Daltons, the Whitmans, the Rothschilds. They're the names that dot this column and all society pages, the names of the city's greatest philanthropists…and the source of its juiciest scandals.

And a doozy is brewing. The police are probing into the murder of Claire Colton, who happened to be the best friend of Madison Taylor-Pruitt, the Golden Girl of real estate and sometime arm candy of Ryan Greene. Of course, when Claire started dating Jack wouldn't give her father or Claire her blessing. Selfish girl!

But here's the thing—Claire showed up dead in a warehouse owned by Pruitt & Pruitt! Could Maddy's daddy be responsible? I hear he might be brought in for questioning. If the charges stick, it could be the end of the Pruitt good name. Unless Madison's not revealing everything she knows. Not to worry. This reporter's not afraid to do a little digging!

Available in August 2006 from Silhouette Sensation

The Captive's Return
by Catherine Mann
(Wingmen Warriors)

The Sheikh Who Loved Me
by Loreth Anne White

Melting Point
by Debra Cowan
((The Hot Zone)

Her Kind of Trouble
by Evelyn Vaughn
(Bombshell)

Secrets of the Wolf
by Karen Whiddon
(The Pack)

The Golden Girl
by Erica Orloff
(Bombshell)

The Golden Girl
ERICA ORLOFF

First published in Great Britain 2006
Silhouette Books, Eton House, 18-24 Paradise Road,
Richmond, Surrey TW9 1SR

© Harlequin Books S.A. 2005

Special thanks and acknowledgement are given to Erica Orloff for her contribution to THE IT GIRLS series.

Standard ISBN 0 373 51372 0
Promotional ISBN 0 373 60478 5

18-0806

Printed and bound in Spain
by Litografia Rosés S.A., Barcelona

ERICA ORLOFF

is a native New Yorker who relocated to sunny South Florida after vowing to never again dig her car out of the snow. She loves playing poker—a Bombshell trait—and likes her martinis dry. Visit her website at www.ericaorloff.com.

Dedicated to Alexa and Isabella, who will always be my very own beloved It Girls.

Acknowledgements

I'd like to thank my agent, Jay Poynor, as always. I'd also especially like to thank my editors, including Margaret Marbury, Natashya Wilson and Julie Barrett, as well as the other wonderful Bombshell authors in this new series.

A thank-you to my family and friends— you know who you are after all this time: Alexa, Nicholas, Isabella, Walter, Maryanne, Kathy J, Kathy L, Pammie, Gina, Jon, Kerri, Cleo and Nanc. And as always, to JD.

Chapter 1

"**P**lease tell me that isn't a thong," Madison Taylor-Pruitt said, rolling her eyes and leaning in to talk to her friend, Ashley Thompson, over the din of Echo, Manhattan's hottest club of the moment.

"Okay, Maddie, I won't tell you." Ash laughed. "But it is."

The two of them were in the VIP room of the club, along with a high-wattage assortment of hip-hop stars, A-list actresses, a handful of supermodels and, unfortunately, the thong-wearing Charlotte "Kiki" Davis. Actually, Maddie thought, thinking of her *own* underwear choice, it wasn't the thong-*wearing* that was so pathetic, it was the thong-*revealing* that made her crazy. Kiki gave Maddie, and every other heiress in New York City, a bad name.

There was a time, she mused, sipping her Cristal champagne, when being an heiress meant discretion. Her mother, the French actress Chantal Taylor, raised her with that in mind. But thanks to a few too many reality shows, and a high-visibility lifestyle, the names that tantalized New York's gossip columns were now just as likely to be listed with a juicy scandal and a major dose of sex appeal as A-list balls and fund-raisers.

Ashley, a fashion editor for *Chic* magazine, hated the trend as much as Maddie. They were both members of the Gotham Roses, an elite group of old-money debs plucked by Renee Dalton-Sinclair, a beautiful society-page regular with a fresh approach to charity work. The Gotham Roses were women who raised *millions* combined for their chosen charities. Maddie loved the work she did for hers—a Spanish Harlem charter school. But heiresses like Kiki, who regularly made "Page Six" and "In the Know with Rubi Cho" with antics in bathroom stalls of nightclubs, and stumbling, breast- and thong-exposing escapades made it seem like all the young and privileged did was party and seek attention.

Maddie's appearances at nightclubs were infrequent at best. She was president of the real-estate division of Pruitt & Pruitt, Inc., a corporation founded by her robber baron great-grandfather before the stock market crash and Great Depression. Pruitt & Pruitt was now synonymous with the Manhattan skyline and real estate—and just about any other industry her father could sink money and talent into—from hotels to shipping to high-tech. So, despite her bikini-perfect figure, her tumbling locks of golden hair, and eyes the society pages described as a cross between blue and green and yellow (depending on whether she was wearing emeralds, sapphires or yellow diamonds with her gowns), Maddie, on any given night, was more likely to be poring over contracts than partying—but Ash was sometimes irresistible, and this Thursday night Maddie had made an exception.

Maddie surveyed the dancing and chaos with a bemused eye and bobbed her head in time to a Moby techno beat. Ash suddenly elbowed her.

"Ryan Greene is making a beeline for the one woman in Manhattan he can't bed."

Maddie looked up and saw Ryan coming toward

her. She shook her head with a slight smile on her face. He never gave up. Her chief rival for every scrap of land or skyscraper she tried to buy, he was convinced the two of them, together, would be the perfect Manhattan dynasty.

Ryan made it to their table and slid next to Maddie on the deep purple velvet couch she was sitting on.

"Hi, Maddie." He smiled, revealing a perfect set of pearly whites Maddie knew only a visit to Dr. Harry March, dentist to the rich and famous, could provide. Ryan had toothpaste-commercial teeth—as perfect as any Hollywood star's. He coupled that with four-hundred-dollar haircuts for his highlighted blond hair, perfectly tailored Italian suits, a Rolex, and a physique toned by, he'd told her more than once, 5:00 a.m. workouts. He was as driven as she was, relentlessly worked as many hours as she did. And he always smelled of a fantastic cologne she could never identify—and refused to ask about.

"Ryan." She smiled enigmatically and nodded.

He leaned in close, his breath hot on her ear. "Care to dance?"

Maddie looked at Ash out of the corner of her eye and gave a shrug. "Sure, why not?"

She put down her champagne glass, winked at

Ash, and allowed Ryan to take her hand. She was wearing the black Chanel suit skirt she'd worn to work—but she had changed in the bathroom of her office to a silk camisole top in a champagne color that almost looked nude. Her shoulders were creamy white, and she knew when Ryan was within touching distance of her, he would go crazy. He always did. That was as predictable as the fact that in the boardroom he was ruthless. Like her father.

They started dancing, and as she expected, he moved very close to her.

"You're wearing that perfume again."

She nodded. It was Sung, and it had a hint of gardenia to it.

"You make me nuts, Maddie. When are you going to come to your senses and realize we're perfect for each other?"

"Never, Ryan." She leaned in close to his ear and flirtatiously nibbled at it. "We'd eat each other alive if we got together, and you know it."

He groaned and then pulled her to him, grinding into her ever so slightly as the pulse of the music got even more erotic.

"Is that a bankbook in your pocket, or are you just happy to see me," she purred.

"You know it's that I'm always happy to see you."

"Along with every other blonde in your zip code."

"You delight in tormenting me, don't you?" He planted a kiss in her neck. "You're the *only* blonde I'm interested in. You know, if we got together, we wouldn't even need a prenup. Then all the buildings we created could be called Greene & Pruitt Towers."

"You mean Pruitt & Greene."

"There's that competitive spirit I love."

A couple of minutes later, the song ended, and the DJ slid into another one, a hip-hop tune requested, as the DJ said into his microphone, by Kiki, who was now dancing on a table, along with a B-list movie actress who apparently had gotten brand-new implants. If her breasts were any higher, Maddie mused, they'd be in her neck like twin goiters.

She and Ryan sat back down with Ash. No sooner had they than gossip columnist Rubi Cho approached them. Rubi, for all the blind items and salacious tidbits she printed, was actually someone Maddie didn't mind. She loved her sense of humor.

"What sexy blond queen of New York real estate was spotted canoodling on the dance floor with her equally sexy male counterpart?" Rubi teased, pushing her purple cat's-eye glasses on top of her shiny black hair.

"You print it, and I'll sue you, Cho," Ryan

growled playfully. "Come on and sit down." He winked at her.

Maddie and Ash waved. Maddie, given how rarely she got to party, rarely made "In the Know with Rubi Cho," but Ryan's dalliances with supermodels and actresses and even a presidential candidate's daughter, often made the Cho column. Maddie hated publicity—but she thought Ryan secretly liked being known as a player. He ate up attention as voraciously as he acquired real estate.

"There goes Kiki's thong," Rubi remarked dryly, and sure enough, the drunken heiress had now removed her thong entirely and was swinging it above her head. "She's a class act. Bet Daddy's real proud at how well finishing school paid off for her."

Ryan, Ash and Maddie all laughed, and Ryan reached over to the ice bucket and refilled their champagne glasses, signaling a cocktail waitress to bring them two more glasses and another bottle of Cristal.

"This is it for me," Maddie said. "I'm driving."

Ryan shook his head. "I don't get it. You must be the only woman worth a hundred million in this town who *drives* herself around. Your father gives you a limo and driver, why don't you use it? You can't tell me you like fighting cabbies for the right-of-way."

Maddie shrugged. "I use the limo most days. It's just…I don't know, sometimes I like to take a drive and clear my head. I'm a damn good driver, too." She didn't tell the three at her table that her father had her learn to drive with the Formula One team he sponsored. She loved speed—and Jack Pruitt believed if you were going to learn to do something, you learned from the best. She took tennis lessons from the coach for the Davis Cup when she was fifteen.

On the small table where her glass rested sat her cell phone. She saw it light up and read the caller ID. Her father's unlisted home phone flashed in digital numbers. That was odd. He rarely called her after nine. She looked at her watch. Twelve-thirty.

She lifted her phone and opened it, holding it to her ear.

"Hello?" she shouted above the nightclub din.

"Maddie?" her father shouted. "Can you hear me?"

"Not really."

"Where are you?"

"Echo. A club."

"Get out."

"What?"

"Get out now! I can't explain. Get out and go home, and I'll call you there and explain."

"But—"

"Get out, Maddie!" Click. He hung up on her.

Puzzled, Maddie closed her phone and smiled at her friends, pretending all was good. "Um…something's come up at the office, of all things. I have to run."

She leaned over and kissed a perturbed-looking Ash on the cheek. Ash asked, "You okay, Maddie?"

She nodded. "Work. You know how insane my schedule gets when I've got a deal pending." She smiled with an assurance she didn't feel. Then Ryan kissed her goodbye as she slid past him, his lips lingering on hers for a fraction of a second. Maddie gave Rubi a peck as she stood up, and then grabbed her purse and cell phone and made her way through the crowded club to the street outside, trying to push down the nervous feeling in her stomach. Her father was considered one of the smartest, most coolheaded and absolutely toughest CEOs in the world. He wasn't prone to emotional reactions—or panic. Not even when the bottom fell out of the stock market years before.

As Maddie exited Echo and walked east the two blocks to her car, a paparazzi photographer snapped her picture.

"Hey, Maddie, real-estate princess, how 'bout smiling for the cameras?"

She glanced over her shoulder and gave a smile, but then a chill ran through her. As if on cue, at the photographer shouting her name, ten guys with cameras suddenly went nuts. Yes, she was well known—but she wasn't Kiki—and she wasn't a supermodel. So the reaction was way out of proportion to her celebrity. Four of them started in a half jog toward her.

"Any comment, Madison?"

"Yeah, what do you have to say?"

She had no idea what the hell was going on—but she was getting out of there. She broke into a half jog, regretting the four-inch heels. She could hear the footfall of the paparazzi behind her, and the *click-click-click* of their shutters going off rapid-fire. She felt like a stalked animal in the wild. Spotting her two-seater Jaguar a few yards up, she pulled the keys from her purse and pressed the button to unlock the doors and turn on the lights. Just a half block ahead of them, she opened the door to her car, hopped in and thanked sheer luck that left enough room around her car for her to pull from the curb in one swift movement once the keys were in the ignition. Still, the photographers snapped away as she drove off down the street.

In her rearview mirror, she could now see two photographers climb into a black Jeep Cherokee and start to pursue her.

"This is insane," she muttered to herself. She was smart enough to know something was up, but she remained utterly in the dark about what it was. All she knew was she didn't relish the photographers catching up to her and nearly ramming her bumper for a better shot. She'd heard of it happening—she had mourned with everyone else in the world at the loss of Princess Diana. Maddie was American royalty, and she didn't want to end up in a crash.

The streets of New York were still busy, but certainly quieter than the bustle of midday or rush hour. She drove several blocks until she pulled onto Fifth Avenue, a shopping mecca with wide streets. She decided she would take it until she could cut over a few cross streets and take a pass through Central Park. If the lights were in her favor, she just might outrun them.

Maddie gripped the steering wheel and spun, making a light and turning toward the park. She could see in her side-view mirror that not only had the photographers not made the light—they didn't care. They blew right through it.

"What the hell is going on that makes me such a hot news topic?" Maddie mused aloud sarcastically. Her tires screeched as she rounded another turn, making an illegal right on red.

The photographers stayed on her, and she could actually glimpse the flash going off as one of them leaned out his window and snapped.

Maddie spied the park in the distance, by the Museum of Natural History entrance, and she tore around a corner, hit a pothole—a deep one—lost a hubcap and drove into the park.

"Yeah!" She smiled to herself. Her rolling hubcap caused the photographers to swerve and jump the curb. With the sidewalk empty at this hour, she was relieved no one was hit, but pleased she'd slowed them down.

Maddie was grateful she had learned to drive like a pro—and that she enjoyed it enough to have spent hours tooling up to one of her family's estates in Saratoga Springs, speeding her way up the thruway and down miles of country roads in her first car—a shiny red BMW. Every year, on her birthday, her father used to surprise her by trading in one car for another. Of course, once she was on her own, she started choosing for herself. Though people often complained of the electrical systems in British cars, she was partial to the Jaguar—and hadn't had one that disappointed her yet.

Maddie picked up speed in the park, passing the occasional nocturnal jogger, and swerving around a horse and carriage with a liveryman and two love-birds in it.

She checked her rearview mirror again and could see the headlights of what she presumed was the photographers' car gaining on her. She inhaled sharply, concentrating, though her mind was moving at warp speed, and her reflexes seemed to be in charge.

She sped through the night, illegally passing a Yellow Cab. The photographers did the same. As she came out the other side of Central Park, she could now see the flashing lights of a cop car bringing up the rear.

"Good," she said aloud to herself, hoping the photographers would pull over. She sure as hell wouldn't. And if she did, wasn't stalking a crime?

Eventually, the photographers did pull over. Maddie guessed they felt they had enough pictures—and a hell of a chase story to regale the tabloids with.

She calmly pulled onto the street and cut down a side street—she didn't even look at the sign. Then she got her bearings and made her way around the out-skirts of the park to her apartment on Central Park West.

Maddie pulled into the underground garage. She climbed out and left the keys in the ignition.

"Hello, Eddie." She smiled at the parking atten-dant.

"Hello, Ms. Pruitt," Eddie said, his uniform crisp, his manner professional, as he held open her door and waited to drive the Jag to its assigned spot.

She nodded at him and took her purse from the passenger seat, grabbing her cell phone. "Oh…damn… um, I lost a hubcap. Can you call the dealer and ar-range for a new one?"

"Sure thing."

Maddie entered the building on the garage level, and pressed a button for the elevator. She could see security cameras watching her from a half-dozen angles. Security was one of her father's pet peeves, among others. Pruitt Towers were not only impec-cable—with marble floors and original paintings in the common areas—but they were the safest build-ings in Manhattan.

When the brass elevator door opened, the eleva-tor operator, Harry, gave a tip of his cap. She smiled at him, stepped into the elevator, and needed to say nothing as he pressed the button for the penthouse. Everyone—from the doormen to housekeeping—knew exactly which apartment belonged to Madison Taylor-Pruitt. The penthouse with the best view of the park.

She got off on her floor and walked to her apartment door, letting herself in and deactivating the alarm. Then she reset for "home," meaning all doors and external windows were secure, but she could roam the apartment at will.

Maddie pressed a button on the wall, and with a nearly silent *whoosh,* all the panels of blinds ascended, revealing a bank of windows with the most incredible view of the park. She admired the twinkling skyline. Then she massaged her neck and slipped off her shoes. It had been a long day—and a long and strange night.

She walked in bare-stocking feet over to the telephone and dialed her father.

"Dad?"

"Maddie. You're safe?"

"Other than being nearly driven off the road by paparazzi. What the hell is going on?"

"Have you turned on the television yet?"

"No."

"You better sit down."

"Dad…" He rarely patronized her, and she abhorred when he did. "Just tell me."

"All right…. It's Claire. She was found murdered tonight."

Chapter 2

"Maddie? Maddie? You still there?"

"Yeah...I'm here," she whispered. She walked to the kitchen and turned on the lights. Custom cherrywood cabinets reflected the halogen lamps hanging from the ceiling. She stepped over to the sink—an immense double one carved from a single piece of granite. Taking a crystal glass from the cabinet, she turned on the tap fitted with a water filter and filled the glass with water.

"Maddie...the police will likely want to interview you tomorrow."

She sipped the water, then stuck her fingers under the faucet, wet her hand and patted her head, feeling mildly dizzy.

"Me? Why?"

"You were her best friend."

"Not in a while, Dad. We hadn't spoken in months." She didn't need to add *thanks to you.*

"Are you going to be okay?"

"No." She wanted to add, *I'll never be okay again.* "How was she…" Maddie couldn't say the words.

"She was shot in a warehouse. The old abandoned one we were looking to buy for the condo project."

"What was she doing there?"

"I have no idea."

"Did she tell you she was going there?" Maddie snapped at her father.

"Is that an accusation?"

"No…" She softened a bit. "I just don't understand."

"Neither do I."

Maddie heard his voice catch a bit, and she wanted to suggest that maybe she take a walk the five blocks to his apartment—a two-story penthouse world famous for its luxury. Then her anger got the best of her.

"I need to go."

"You want me to come over?"

"No, Dad. In fact, right about now, you're the last person I want to see." She hung up the phone abruptly, her hands shaking slightly.

Maddie walked through the living room to her cavernous master bedroom. She'd furnished it with an immense four-poster antique bed, its headboard intricately carved sometime during the Victorian era. Egyptian-cotton sheets in a pristine ivory shade and modern touches in the room, including a haunting black-and-white photo by Diane Arbus and a painting by Julian Schnabel, made it seem very fresh, though. Maddie moved to an armoire in the corner of the room and opened the double doors, pulling out a drawer. There, nestled in among her silk camisoles, was a small wooden box. She took it out and sat down on her bed, opening the lid.

Her first instinct, all those months ago, had been to rip up her pictures and memories, to pretend she'd never known Claire. Now, her once–best friend murdered in cold blood, she was grateful she hadn't. She pulled out a photo of the two of them, smiling, on a trip through Napa Valley wine country. They were on horseback—Maddie remembered Claire's mount nearly bucked her off. Next was a photo of them in Paris, when Maddie's mother had flown them there for a weekend of art and gourmet meals. It had been unseasonably cold, and Claire's black hair framed her face in a classic Clara Bow bob. She looked like a 1930s movie star, with her Kewpie doll lips and big black eyes. But woe to anyone who doubted her ability in the courtroom. In the picture, Maddie stood next to Claire, her polar opposite in terms of looks. Both of them had on hats and scarves to ward off the chill. They had asked a handsome Frenchman to snap their photo, and he had captured them midlaugh.

Maddie stared at the photos. Claire had been so much a part of her life—her first friend at boarding school. After high school, they'd gone to Harvard together, roomed together, gotten an apartment together. She hadn't imagined a time when they wouldn't be together. But that was before the dinner nearly six months ago that changed her entire world....

"How's your soufflé?" her father asked her.

"Excellent."

"And yours, Claire?"

Claire nodded, but despite her friend's famous sweet tooth, Maddie had noticed how she'd just picked at her dessert.

They were seated in the upstairs dining room of 412—an exclusive restaurant in Manhattan so pricey and discreet that it was simply known by the number on its door, and no other markings delineated it as a restaurant. Its number was unlisted. The upstairs dining room was for the clientele even an establishment like 412 distinguished as the most elite of the elite. Jack Pruitt and his daughter, Maddie, were regulars.

"Maddie," her father began. "You know I would never hurt you for anything in the world.…" He hesitated and sipped at his Glenfiddich on the rocks. His sandy blond hair was streaked with an elegant silver, though it was still full and thick. His broad shoulders and wrinkleless skin made him appear ten or even twenty years younger. "But sometimes, just like in business, things happen. They're not personal, but people do get hurt."

Maddie felt the color drain from her face. Something was very wrong when Jack Pruitt, who prided himself on having the charm of a showman mixed with the coldness of a viper, began talking about feelings. It wasn't the Pruitt style.

"So," he continued, "there's no way to say this gracefully. Claire and I have fallen in love."

"What?" Maddie looked at Claire. "When? I mean…God…what? Claire, you've mentioned nothing to…" But Maddie's question had stopped as the previous few months swirled around her. All Claire's late nights with her father, ostensibly going over the latest legal filings. She'd joined Pruitt & Pruitt as in-house counsel, and Maddie had felt relieved at first that there was someone in the legal department she and her father could trust implicitly. Now she felt like a fool. Her supposed best friend had been sleeping with her father. It felt so sordid.

Maddie pulled her chair back from the table, as Claire, usually so eloquent, stammered, "Please, Maddie…we didn't even realize it was happening at first. It started innocently, I swear to you."

"Nothing," Maddie whispered as she rose stiffly from the table, "is innocent. We're all grown-ups, but don't insult my intelligence. At some point during your affair, each of you had a time when you could have stopped and said that it wasn't worth betraying me. Or you could have told me when it started, not hid it, lying to my face. But both of you carried on. For that, I can never forgive either of you."

She gathered her purse and suit jacket and left the two of them in stunned silence.

Maddie shut her eyes at the memories. That Monday, at the office, Claire had desperately tried to see her. She'd dropped by Maddie's office, her dark eyes welling slightly when she looked at Maddie's desk and saw that all the photo frames of the two of them—and Maddie's father—had been put away. Maddie had cut her friend from her life. Her father, she had to deal with professionally. But even that relationship had grown chillier. Of course, the ever-confident swagger of Jack Pruitt never faltered—and he never apologized or raised the issue with his daughter again. He and Claire became a visible couple, and all of the city—especially the gossip columnists—had buzzed. Had the beautiful corporate attorney, decades his junior, finally snagged the most eligible bachelor in New York? Could Maddie's closest confidante end up her stepmother?

Maddie winced at the memories and rose from her bed and went to the bedroom window, looking out on Manhattan, the city whose skyline she was helping to shape with her real-estate ventures. The waterfront warehouse where her father said Claire was killed was in New Jersey—and it offered a spectacular view of Manhattan across the waters of the Hudson River. Maddie had been bidding against Ryan Greene, her real-estate nemesis and flirting friend, for the land. But there was no reason for Claire to have been there. In fact, aside from Madi-

son and Jack Pruitt, few ever knew for sure of the
hush-hush dealings of Pruitt & Pruitt's real-estate division. They were secretive because as soon as word
got out as to what they were bidding on, competi-
tors rushed to vie for the same building or land. But
whoever had murdered Claire knew about the warehouse—and Claire knew about it, albeit without her
needing to visit it.

Maddie puzzled over this. Who would have suggested meeting Claire there? Who did Claire trust
enough to meet in an abandoned warehouse?
Though Maddie thought her father was capable of
many things, murder wasn't one of them. But she
knew that wouldn't stop him from being suspect
number one when the police looked into the slaying
of the beautiful Claire Shipley, his much-younger
lover.

Chapter 3

"Madison, darling?"

"Yes?" Maddie said into her private cell phone and sipped her coffee. Her voice was raspy from lack of sleep.

"Renee."

"Hi, Renee…" Madison said a bit unsteadily. Renee had recruited her into the prestigious Gotham Roses, appealing to her sense of philanthropy. The Pruitt Family Trust was known for doling out millions of dollars in charity each year—and Madison was instrumental in choosing the charities. But

Gotham Roses was more personal—a chance to actually go out and do something for the charity of her choice. Nonetheless, she and Renee were acquaintances only. And now, Madison guessed that she quite possibly was about to be kicked out of the Gotham Roses for dragging their name through the mud. Already the front pages of the two major New York daily papers were covering the murder—and her father's affair with her former best friend—in gory detail.

"I'm so, so sorry to read of your friend's murder."

"Thank you," Madison murmured.

"Is there anything I can do?"

"No. I'm skipping the office today and working from my home—the better to avoid the phalanx of reporters outside my place. Two nearly ran me off the road last night."

"They can be awful.... I felt like they were a school of sharks encircling me during Preston's trial six years ago," Renee said sympathetically, referring to her husband who Renee always maintained had been framed for financial misdealings at his family's investment company. "Do you think you can slip away, though?"

Here it comes, Madison thought. "Sure, Renee."

"Wonderful. I'll expect you for tea then, whenever you can get here."

Madison hung up. She had told her housekeeper, who usually came twice a week, to stay home. A pot of coffee sat on the corner of her desk, and Maddie had been drinking cup after cup of the French roast. She hadn't slept at all the previous night, tossing and turning and sighing. She wasn't the crying sort—she had been raised to be coolheaded. But her heart ached.

Maddie rose from her desk and stretched. She hadn't needed to dress in her usual office attire. She most often favored Chanel suits, or black classic suits from other designers, with silk blouses—always with feminine details, whether that meant a sexier cut, or unusual buttons, or French cuffs. She liked heels that raised her from her usual five foot seven to close to five foot eleven. She mused that if you wanted to play tough in New York City real estate with the big boys, you had better be able to look them in the eye.

"Casual Friday"—and today was Friday—meant nothing to Madison. She had power lunches and meetings every single day, and she never wanted to look less than her professional best. But today, working from home, she wore her typical weekend attire—Donna Karan—who had once espoused that one of the most essential wardrobe pieces was the simple black bodysuit. Maddie wore a black Karan bodysuit, dark blue jeans, loafers and a simple black sweater. For color, she wore a necklace with a large amethyst—her birthstone.

Sighing, Madison looked at her watch. It was two. She dreaded seeing Renee, expecting to be "called on the carpet." The Gotham Roses were supposed to represent the stars of philanthropy. White-collar crime was one thing. Murder another. But Maddie felt it best to get it over with. She was practical that way. She never felt it was worth putting off the inevitable. The police were scheduled to interview her at six that evening, which gave her plenty of time to get to the Gotham Roses Club on the Upper East Side, at Sixty-eighth between Park and Madison, and back again.

She called down to the garage and told them to have her limo and driver ready. With its black-tinted windows, Maddie knew the photographers clustered outside would snap away, but she would be safely ensconced from their sight inside.

She took another gulp of coffee, left her office, grabbed her purse from the dining-room table, set the alarm code at the door and descended in the elevator to the basement.

Her limo was waiting, and her driver, Charlie,

gave her a small smile, worry etched on his face. He had been her personal driver since her parents divorced when she was twelve. Charlie was the one to ferry her between the warring Jack Pruitt and Chantal Taylor, taking her from one penthouse to the other across Central Park, her beloved cat—and goldfish, Sam—in tow. Charlie was a former marine, who'd done a couple of tours in Vietnam. When her father hired him, Charlie had been putting his life back together again after his wife left him, starting with quitting drinking. He was older now, his hair streaked with gray. But Maddie knew, gray hair and bum right knee aside, he was loyal enough to do anything to keep her safe. And he was equally loyal to Jack Pruitt, who gave him a chance when no one else had.

Charlie held open the door for her, and she slid into the back, the leather seats smooth against her touch. She smiled. Next to her usual seat in the back was a copy of the latest issue of *Forbes*. He knew her so well. Usually, he'd also have a copy of the morning's *New York Reporter*, opened to the "In the Know with Rubi Cho" column. Charlie knew her newspaper reading at the office was limited to the *Times* and the *Wall Street Journal*, but he and Maddie would chuckle over the innuendos and blind items about people they knew in Rubi's column. Today, no *Reporter* waited for her, because, she was sure, the murder was on page one and would fill the gossip columns for weeks. He would instinctively protect her from that.

"I'm going to the Gotham Roses Club, Charlie," she said when he got behind the wheel. "Just wait for me when we get there. I shouldn't be all that long, and then I have to get back here…the police are coming to interview me about Claire."

"I'm really sorry, Miss Madison."

"Me, too, Charlie. Me, too."

She settled back into the plush seat and shut her eyes, actually dozing for a few minutes on the way to the club. She felt the car stop and opened her eyes.

The Gotham Roses Club was in a beautiful brownstone with a white facade, wrought-iron gate, and a feel about it that said old-money establishment, gentility, quiet wealth. She loved the building—had since the first time she laid eyes on it a year before.

While she and her father prided themselves on some of the most spectacular high-rises and lofts in New York, she did love the feeling of the old brownstones near embassy row, an area of New York where many consulates and embassies quietly maintained their headquarters. The streets were quieter, tree-lined, and seemed from another time.

Charlie got out and held open the door for her. She patted his arm and smiled at him as she got out, reassuring him she'd be okay. She went to the gate and pressed a buzzer. When she gave her name, she was buzzed in immediately after looking up at the security camera.

Entering the club made the bustle of New York seem even more distant than the tree-lined street on the Upper East Side had. In the immense entrance hall, Debussy was piped in through hidden speakers, and immediately Maddie felt a tiny bit of tension leave her shoulders. The floors were polished parquet in an intricate pattern, the workmanship definitely from the Roaring Twenties. A grand staircase swept up to the second floor, curving, with a carved banister in rosewood. Curtains covered the windows and puddled on the floor, creating an ambience that was elegant yet relaxed, with sunlight streaming through their filmy whiteness. A fireplace huge enough to stand inside took up a portion of the wall to the left, and as always in the fall, a toasty fire glowed.

Olivia Hayworth, Renee's personal secretary,

greeted her warmly, kissing her on each cheek. "So glad you could make the trip in these circumstances, Madison. Please let me know if there's anything we can do. We've sent over flowers to the funeral home, and the Shipley family listed a charity—"

"Yes, they give a great deal to the Children's Museum in Philadelphia. Claire had a niece who had leukemia—since recovered. The museum was Amy's favorite place during treatment and afterward."

"Well, we've sent a sizable donation, in the Club's name."

"Thank you, truly. That's very thoughtful. I'll let my father know. I'm sure he'll appreciate your gesture."

"Renee's waiting for you in the sunroom. Tea will be served in just a few minutes now that you're here."

Madison nodded and made her way down the hallway to the sunroom in the back of the brownstone. The French doors were open and there sat Renee Dalton-Sinclair, her auburn hair in an elegant bun, and dressed to perfection in an Oscar de la Renta suit. She rose and extended her hand. Though Madison knew she was in her forties, her beauty was timeless in a Grace Kelly sort of way.

"Hello, Madison. Thank you so much for coming." Renee leaned forward and kissed Madison's cheek as the two women clasped hands.

"Good to see you."

"Again, I am so sorry…terrible, terrible crime."

Madison nodded. It was difficult accepting condolences when she knew that as much as Claire had hurt her, she had wounded Claire in return by refusing to forgive her.

"Sit down. How are you feeling?"

Madison was unused to making more than small talk with Renee, but she was also weary. She opened up a bit.

"To be honest…awful. I haven't slept." Madison ran her fingers through her long golden-blond hair. "And…Claire and I had a falling-out over her relationship with my father. They had hidden it for months, and…well, it was hard to accept. So I feel terrible that she's gone and things hadn't been right between us."

Renee nodded, her royal-blue eyes conveying empathy.

"Anyway," Madison said, waving a hand, "the Pruitts are nothing if not tough. It's just going to be rough going for a little while."

Renee pursed her lips and clasped her hands together. She gave a nearly imperceptible nod and one of her staff wheeled in a tea cart with a beautiful bone china tea set on it. Madison was always amazed at how Renee's crew forgot nothing. There were two hundred members of the Gotham Roses, but Maddie assumed the staff kept a catalog of each member's likes and dislikes, because without asking, she got a cup of Earl Grey tea with lemon, no sugar, no cream—exactly as she liked it. The woman also handed her a plate with two scones on it, and raspberry jam as opposed to strawberry—also her preference.

After the woman had served Renee, she retreated from the sunroom, shutting the French doors behind her.

"Madison, perhaps you're wondering why I've brought you here in the midst of your crisis."

Madison nodded, ready for the worst.

"Well, the police are making vague references to 'persons of interest.' Of course, your father heads that list."

"I know," Madison said softly.

"Well…I consider myself an excellent judge of character. If I wasn't, I couldn't have created this charitable organization. In the year you've been a Gotham Rose, you've always struck me as a bit aloof, a shrewd negotiator. Cautious, perhaps, in your personal life. You stay out of the headlines—except when you think it counts, namely well-executed business deals. You are absolutely driven, the kind of person who thrives on putting in a hundred and fifty percent and the thrill of the deal."

"I think that's a fair assessment."

"And my guess is being the by-product of the most famous divorce in New York history is part of that. At twelve, your life was an open book, wasn't it? That's why you guard your privacy."

Maddie sighed. "They fought over every detail. My mother had to have a private chef shuttle between my father's household and mine so that she could control what I ate—macrobiotic. When I got to college, I had my first taste of caffeine and loved it." She smiled at the memory, but then shook her head. "I had matching wardrobes at her apartment and his. My father was required to send me on vacations tallying no less than twenty-five thousand dollars a year. I had to have two nannies at each home—a morning nanny, who also got me from school and oversaw homework—and a night nanny. It was insane. I was branded the Poor Little Rich Girl. They used to snap pictures of me getting out of my limo at school, with the headline Hundred-Million-Dollar Baby."

Renee nodded. "Then there was that brilliant IQ of yours. Skipping grades. Private tutors to challenge you. Fluent in three languages. And finally, there are the things no one knows…like your training."

Maddie looked at Renee, puzzled. "My training?"

Renee smiled enigmatically. "You can fire a .44 better than an FBI sharpshooter. And I believe you know the correct technique to break a man's nose—or even kill him—with just the right palm-to-face blow."

"I don't understand…that stuff isn't anything I would ever discuss with anyone. No one knows outside my father and the men he had train me."

"I know. And why did he train you?"

"Well," Maddie said coolly, "you seem to know so much about me, why don't *you* tell me?"

"Trust me in that this all will make sense in a few minutes. From what I understand, your father and his brother Bing were actually two of three brothers. And the middle brother, William, was kidnapped and died in a botched rescue attempt. Though that was covered up by the family so that their failed security wouldn't seem like an invitation to every kidnapper in the world back then to try again."

Maddie stared incredulously. "Yes, though I'm…

I don't know what to say. Yes, that's true. Understandably, my father has a security obsession. He wanted me to be safe, but then he knew that even a personal-security detail could have failings— namely, traitors. So he wanted me to be able to defend myself. It might seem a bit extreme, but I was trained by former Black Ops. Two of them who own a private security firm… Look, Renee, what is all this about?"

"It's about me wanting to know what makes Madison Taylor-Pruitt tick. Madison, do you believe your father had nothing to do with Claire's death?"

"Absolutely."

"Then why was she shot at a property your father was negotiating for?"

"I don't know. What I do know is I want the killer or killers brought to justice soon, because she was my friend, and because this kind of publicity Pruitt & Pruitt can do without."

"What if I was to say I can offer you the chance to do just that?"

"Just what?"

"Find the killer. Would the Madison Taylor-Pruitt I think I know—nerves of steel and a resolve unlike anyone else's—would she take me up on the offer?"

"Yes. Though I don't know how you can offer

that, so it's a hypothetical, Renee." Madison lifted her teacup and sipped, and then took a bite of her scone.

"Madison, the Gotham Roses was an idea close to my heart. In my wilder youth, I was in the Peace Corps—that's where Olivia and I met, you know—and I saw firsthand what good people with high ideals can do. But after I married Preston, I also saw what ruthless people with low ideals can do. The Sinclair family, his own flesh and blood, took advantage of his honesty and decency, and they framed him, made him a scapegoat. It nearly destroyed me. Until I received my own unusual offer—similar to the one I am making you today."

"An offer?"

Renee nodded. "An offer to go undercover."

"What? You mean, like for the police?"

"That's exactly what I mean. It would provide you with a chance to clear your father's name—and find Claire's killer."

"I'd do it."

"Don't say yes quite so fast."

"I'm used to making split-second decisions based on my gut."

"This is a bit more elaborate. You'd be working for a cover agency—not the police per se. You'd have to decide for sure that you'd be willing to dedicate yourself to catching the real killer, and sign an oath of allegiance that, if broken, would be just as serious as breaking an oath to the FBI or CIA. So think about it carefully."

"If I can commit a hundred million dollars to a new waterfront high-rise and steam ahead with it in the face of every obstacle a large-scale building project can have, I can commit to this, Renee."

"I knew I could count on you. And frankly, dear, you have too much to lose not to take me up on this, shall we say, opportunity."

Renee paused, then continued, "When Preston had his legal issues, I was contacted by a woman named the Governess. Never directly, though we've spoken on the phone. Through representatives. And this person—and even I'm unsure who she is—wields unprecedented power. You, your father, Preston, myself, we deal with money and boardrooms and power. But this is power with the strength of the government and FBI behind it—resources I still find amazing."

Madison tried to follow what Renee was driving at. "Are you saying you work for the government?"

"In a manner of speaking, yes. The offer—early release for Preston—came with strings attached. I considered the strings positive, however. I never lost that part of me who was the free-spirited girl in the Peace Corps, determined to do good. The strings involved running a secret organization that reports only to the Governess. With backing and support from the FBI, the CIA and other law-enforcement entities, including Scotland Yard and MI-5, this organization is now embedded in the Gotham Roses. Among you are about fifteen or sixteen handpicked women with talents and ambitions needed to bring down various criminal activities. Undercover."

"But why the Roses? Why not the FBI or the CIA or…the regular police? Why involve a bunch of— no offense—wealthy young women? What do we— or you—bring to the table?"

"Do you know how to use a lobster fork, Madison?"

Maddie laughed a little. "Sure."

"And how to use a finger bowl?"

Maddie nodded.

"Can you waltz, fox-trot, discuss the Bauhaus movement in art and converse with a diplomat—in his or her native language usually?"

"Sure."

"Well, shocking as this may be to you, Madison, this world we live in, this bubble, if you will, isn't easily penetrated. The society pages, for instance, are concerned with *old* money. You and I both know how we often feel about the nouveau riche. The Kikis of the world, the women who, despite the wealth they may have married into, wouldn't know class if it ran them over."

"So?"

Renee leaned forward. "It would be impossible for the FBI or law enforcement to penetrate the society pages, to blend in with us, to fall into step with our world, if they had to solve a crime in our midst. And with Enron, with the various scandals…Tyco… whomever…we're talking some crimes that not only top the hundreds of millions of dollars, but also that trickle down to ordinary people who put their faith in the officers of the board. If they claim the company to be financially sound, the public believes it until a scandal breaks and sends the market tumbling, and suddenly Mr. and Mrs. John Q. Public lose their life savings."

"So you're saying these women have been working as…spies? Cops?"

"Agents. They're able to blend in and solve major financial and banking cases, even drug dealing among the elite. They can do what the FBI can't— namely, infiltrate the path of crime among mind-boggling wealth without being perceived as interlopers."

"I'm…stunned."

"Well, Madison, I always knew you had talents that would put even the best and brightest to shame, but I also knew the best agents have a passion, a reason, for joining. It's a tremendous commitment, and it means a duplicitous life. And it's not something anyone should undertake just because she's an adrenaline junkie or thinks it might be a lark."

"And then Claire was murdered," Maddie whispered.

"Yes. And I wouldn't wish this crisis on my worst enemy, not even on the bastards in the Sinclair family who framed my beloved Pres. But when I saw the news last night, so did the Governess. Madison, rumors are floating that Claire's death is less personal than you may think."

"What do you mean 'less personal'?"

"She may have been murdered to stop her from revealing financial irregularities at Pruitt & Pruitt. And the administration would like to avoid seeing another Enron. The financial markets are unstable enough as they are."

"So you think there is something illegal going on at our company and that Claire was murdered for being a whistle-blower? I can't believe it."

Renee nodded. "What I, or the FBI, think is immaterial. We need facts—and we need you to get them or we'll assign the case to someone else."

"Pruitt & Pruitt is my life. I'm not going to let it be destroyed. If elements in my company are trying to skirt the law, I *will* find out."

"If you want to do this, Madison, you need to show up here tomorrow at 1:00 p.m. and meet your handler. If you don't show, I'll know that it wasn't meant to be. Just as I know you will never speak of this to anyone. Ever. And if you show up, you will be trained even further than your father's private security firm trained you. You'll be pushed to your limit. And I know, of anyone, you'll succeed."

Maddie was still absorbing all Renee had told her. She looked at her watch. "Okay, Renee, I'll think about it. I should go, though. The police want to interview me."

"Of course. I hope I see you tomorrow. I learned a long time ago that we can live life in a gilded cage, or we can live life fully using our talents."

They both stood. Renee clasped Maddie's hand. Then Maddie left the sunroom and headed for her limo.

Charlie held open the door for her. She settled into the back seat and shut her eyes, her head spinning.

"You okay, Miss Madison?"

"Yeah, Charlie. Just have a lot on my mind."

"Want to take a drive out to the country? Leaves are in full fall glory about now."

"No, thanks. I have the police coming at six."

"Right. Okay. Well, you just call my cell phone if you need anything."

"Thanks, Charlie." She smiled, remembering how he sometimes used to sneak her off after school to get ice cream if she'd had a bad day—a direct violation of her mother's macrobiotic rules.

A short time later, Charlie eased the limo into the parking garage. Maddie got out, leaning over the front seat to give him a peck on the cheek first. Once in the building, she pressed the elevator for up and took it to her floor.

Glancing at her watch, Maddie saw she had an hour before the police arrived. She was dreading the interview. She unlocked the door to her place, and turned to her left to deactivate the alarm—only to be hit on the back of her head with something. She guessed the butt of a gun as she saw stars, but she had, through luck or training, "felt" the presence of someone for a split second before she'd fully even processed the thought in her brain. She'd turned just enough to deflect the blow, and though the pain through her neck and shoulder was severe, she hadn't blacked out.

Whirling, she saw a man with a black wool ski

mask. He froze for a second, surprised, she guessed, that she was still standing. She immediately grabbed the seventeenth-century stone statue of a pagoda that rested atop the desk in her entranceway, and swung it for the head of her assailant. She missed but managed to land a solid hit to his shoulder.

"Bitch!" came his muffled response. He reached out, trying to grab her by the throat, but Maddie ducked—always keep them off balance, her martial arts trainer had told her—and then landed a solid punch to his solar plexus.

He doubled over, and she knew she'd knocked the wind out of him. He wheezed and coughed, then raised one fist and punched her in return, landing on her jaw. She flew backward against the wall. Still on her feet, she somehow managed to land a round-house kick into his thigh. Now he was really angry, she could tell.

He bellowed, grabbing her by the hair, and rammed her head against the wall. She finally screamed—loud. She clawed at his mask. But using her hair for leverage of some sort, he spun her away from himself and then dashed out the door and down the hall to the stairwell.

Maddie had fallen back against the sharp point of the corner of her dining-room table. Pain coursed through her back, but she willed herself to get to the keypad of her alarm system. She pressed the panic button, still puzzled as to how the assailant had outwitted her system. The button made the entire keypad light up with red lights. Maddie looked down the hall, the assailant now gone, and waited for the security company to dispatch a team.

Someone, she decided, was up to no good at Pruitt & Pruitt. And she was more determined than ever to figure out who that was.

Chapter 4

The security company was still there when the police arrived. The head of security, Marcus Barron, was taciturn, his face etched with fury. No one outwitted his system—ever.

The two plainclothes detectives gave their names as Tom Briggs and Ed Compton. They talked with Marcus, who kept shaking his head incredulously.

"This guy was not only a pro, disabling a camera in the hall, but he knew the building codes. He didn't set off the alarms, because he knew what codes to use."

"Even to her apartment?"

Marcus nodded.

Briggs, the taller cop, with a build like a former football player, said, "So who has the codes?"

"Our system, in ten years of business, has never been hacked. Ever. I presume the head of the building's security detail is to blame for the breach. I don't know. She says no one has her code—her father insisted on it."

"What about her father?"

"Her own father attacked his daughter? Jack Pruitt? You've got to be kidding me, man."

"Stranger things have happened in our line of work."

"No. You don't think she'd recognize him, even with a ski mask?"

"Then he could have hired someone."

Maddie listened to all this with an ice pack pressed to her neck. "Look, gentlemen, this is all preposterous. I interrupted a thief. Do you have any idea what the art in this apartment is worth? In the millions. That painting—" she swept her hand toward a Picasso "—is worth over a million itself. I inherited it from my grandmother, who was an avid Picasso lover."

Ordinarily, Maddie would never flaunt her wealth

like that, but the two cops were irritating her with their insinuations. And she did think it had to do with Pruitt & Pruitt, but no sense giving the police any idea about her father—he was under a big enough cloud of suspicion already.

Marcus said, "I'm going to post a security detail outside your apartment until we redo the system tomorrow."

"That's not necessary."

Marcus, with the chiseled features of a roman statue and the sculpted body to match, shook his head. "Look, Ms. Pruitt, your father's company pays me a lot of money to keep its valuables safe. And I'd say, if you excuse the expression, you're his most precious possession. You can't talk me out of it, so know our guys are there and then put it from your mind. And I still think you should go to the hospital."

"Dr. Halloway is coming over." He was the Pruitt family's personal physician. She and her father were in superb shape, but Jack Pruitt couldn't tolerate the thought of ever wasting even ten seconds in a doctor's waiting room. So Halloway played a lot of golf and was kept on a retainer basis. He had gone to prep school with Jack Pruitt and her father was extremely loyal to old friends.

Hours later, Maddie was mentally—and physically—exhausted. The police hadn't seemed as interested in catching Claire's killer as in nailing her father. She was used to it in a way. People loved to take down the wealthy, to be able to think, "See, money can't buy you happiness." Maddie knew that was a thousand percent true. Her childhood, for instance, hadn't been a particularly happy one. But she also knew relishing the downfall of another person wasn't right either. By the end of the interview, Detective Briggs had begun zeroing in on Maddie herself—her resentment over her father's affair with Claire. Luckily, Maddie had an airtight alibi. She had been at the office when Claire was killed. After that, she was in the club—and had been seen there by hundreds of people, not to mention she *had* gotten a playful mention in Rubi's column.

Briggs even went so far as to insinuate that Maddie herself had staged the break-in. Maddie had risen from the dining-room table, and with all the iciness she could muster, and with a look in her eyes that would instill panic in even the toughest lawyers negotiating with her over a piece of property, she said, "The mayor will be hearing from me about this ridiculous line of questioning as my friend's body lies in the morgue. You can leave now, gentlemen, and don't come back. If you do, you'll find my attorneys will make you wish you'd never joined the force. If, after my call to the mayor, you even stay detectives instead of being reassigned to the K–9 unit."

After they had left, Halloway had arrived and given her a prescription for an anti-inflammatory and a painkiller. She intended to fill neither. Her father called.

"Marcus filled me in. What the hell happened?"

"If he filled you in, then you know, Dad. Look, I'm wiped out."

"Dammit, Madison, I hate it when you don't keep me informed."

"Hmm… Imagine how I felt about you and Claire. Uninformed, lied to. I'm going to bed. Good night." She hung up. Then Maddie had poured herself a stiff drink and tried to think.

Claire had been an absolute tigress in the courtroom—but she was proud of her reputation. There wasn't any way she had been involved in anything illegal. So who was the traitor at Pruitt & Pruitt? And who was so powerful to have been able to access her building and her apartment?

Maddie sipped her scotch—a single malt that would go for two hundred dollars a shot at any high-end restaurant. She remembered being twenty-three the first time she had scotch. She had thought it was the single most vile drink on the planet, but again, her father had taught her well. The "big boys" she negotiated with and against drank it to celebrate closing a deal—and she learned to drink it, too. Now she enjoyed a smooth scotch—and she needed it to steady her nerves in light of all that had happened in the previous twenty-four hours.

She gazed out on the skyline, and Renee's words rang in her ears. All her life, Madison had wanted to build skyscrapers, to leave her mark in history—on the skyline of Manhattan. She wanted to look out on spires and soaring glass buildings and know she was responsible for making these hundred-million-dollar projects a reality. But as a member of the Gotham Roses undercover organization, she could do so much more. So in the wee hours, as Manhattan spread like a shining jewel in front of her, Madison Taylor-Pruitt decided she would work undercover. She would be a government agent. And she would see that justice was done. For Claire.

Bam!

Madison was flung through the air and to the mat by her trainer. She'd hit the mat so hard, she thought she'd broken a tooth.

Jimmy Valentine gave her a grin and reached a hand down to help her up. Madison actually felt for the mat beneath her. She felt as if she'd hit solid floor, not mat, but no…the mat was still there.

"Man, you are one well-trained lady." Jimmy smiled. "You may be my best agent yet."

Maddie accepted his proffered hand and rose, slowly, from her prone position. "Well trained? You're kicking my ass."

"Look at me. I'm six foot one, a good two hundred twenty-five first thing in the morning before I've eaten my way through one of my wife, Linda's, breakfasts. I *should* be kicking your ass. I'd be kicked out of the CIA if I couldn't. Now let's try that move one more time."

Jimmy was teaching her to do leg sweeps, whereby she literally tried to sweep an opponent's legs out from under him or her. This was after a half hour on a heavy bag, twenty minutes of jump rope, four miles on a treadmill set for steep uphill, and a firearms lesson, which she had passed, Jimmy said, "like you were a born sniper."

Maddie tried to focus, but she was still absorbing the fact that beneath Renee's glamorous home and the Gotham Roses elegant club was a labyrinth of rooms and tunnels. Feeling as if she was in a James

Bond movie, after she was processed and prodded and poked by a doctor, and after her irises were scanned into some high-tech security equipment, which made even what Pruitt & Pruitt had look amateurish, she was ushered downstairs into a whole new world.

Maddie decided the best metaphor for it was an anthill. There may have been a whole world, busy and bustling upstairs in the Club. There were always teas, events, planning meetings and lunches being held to benefit their charities. On the second and third floors were Renee's private residence—just she and her daughter with Preston still in prison. But beneath the world of the hill above was another world. Madison saw two or three fellow Roses turned agents ushered in and out of high-tech rooms, and she discovered, when Renee gave her the tour, that everything from computer equipment to sophisticated listening devices, to a firing range and training center, even to a dressing room with a stylist who helped women when they went under deeper cover, were all housed here.

Most amusing, to Maddie at least, were the people like Jimmy Valentine, who was their trainer. She had seen him before. In a painter's outfit, splattered with the color of Renee's sitting room. Another man she saw tending to an immense computer she had always believed was one of Renee's personal accountants.

"You ready, Pruitt?" Jimmy grinned at her. He was certainly gorgeous, with classic Italian sexiness, but behind that smile was a deadly serious trainer. He showed no mercy because, he said, "The bad guys won't either."

They squared off against each other. Maddie stayed out of the range of his reach—which was the tricky part. He so seriously outsized her that in order for her to attack him, she had to get close to him, which meant he could grab her and send her sailing across the room.

She inhaled deeply through her nostrils. Belly breathing would show him she was tired, which she sure as heck was. But she wasn't about to let Jimmy Valentine know. This was day two of training, and she was determined to take him down.

Get him off guard, she told herself. When she'd trained with her father's Black Ops guys they constantly stressed that hand-to-hand combat was as much a mental game as a physical game.

She suddenly dropped to the floor, slid in close to Jimmy, and with one vicious and fast side-sweep of her long leg, flattened him. Before he could grab her, she'd rolled three times, was up on her feet, and drew her gun—which was unloaded for practice.

"Freeze!"

Jimmy Valentine stared up at the ceiling. She thought she'd really hurt him and dashed over to him.

"You okay?"

He smiled a huge grin, ran his hands through his thick black hair and sat up. "My leg hurts like a son of a bitch, but I'm more than okay. Honey, you are going to surprise a helluva lot of people. Most especially, some bad guys."

"You think?"

"Look, some of the women who are undercover, they're gorgeous. Who am I kidding? They're all knockouts—Vanessa Dawson? She's a goddess. And they're smart, sophisticated. And they can shoot, now that they've been trained. They all have talent. But you have it inbred in you. I read your file. Your father being paranoid about kidnapping and all."

"Yeah. I was already training in my teens, and then got more intense training when I went off to college."

"That's the key. They got you when you were young. It's like second nature. Great drop to the floor. I wasn't expecting it."

He lifted the leg of his black tracksuit. "I'm gonna have a terrific bruise. Good for sympathy from Linda."

"What does she think of your job?"

He shrugged. "As long as I'm safe and come home to my girls at night, she's cool with it. I have two daughters—Mia and Sienna. Apples of my eye."

"Let's try that choke-hold routine again."

"They warned me about you."

"What do you mean?"

"The amazing type-A competitive streak. You're so driven, they say your *blood* is type A."

"Oh, aren't we clever."

"Always, Park Avenue Princess, always," he said, his brown eyes making clear he meant it affectionately.

Jimmy finally stood and said, "You're sure you want to go another round?"

She nodded.

The choke hold involved him facing her and placing his hands around her neck—he didn't apply much pressure, but enough that she had to be cautious to fight panic. Then her move was to jam her forearms up between his two arms and force his arms outward with as strong a motion as she could. The fact that Jimmy's forearms were the size of her thighs made things tricky.

They each readied their stance, and Jimmy pretended to choke her.

Maddie fought against the tide of panic. *It's a mental game,* she told herself, *just like staring down the piranhas who wanted to force the sale of Pruitt's hotel holdings last year.*

In an instant, she flashed back to the masked intruder reaching for her throat. Fear mixed with anger, and she brought her arms up in a swift motion and slammed them against the inner forearms of Jimmy. He grunted, but released her neck, and she took four steps back and pulled her weapon.

"Freeze!"

"Thumbs up! You fight like a champ."

"Thanks." She beamed. He was right. She couldn't help it, but she was competitive to a fault, and knowing she was better than most filled her with pride. Like being valedictorian of her elite private high school—only better. She liked knowing she was trained to do combat. It stirred something inside her.

After she finished with Jimmy, she was brought to the dressing room, which had an adjoining medical room with a massage table and whirlpool spa and other delights for sore muscles. She had no time for a rubdown, though. She showered and changed and was brought to a briefing room. There, she met with Troy Carter, who was assigned to be her handler.

"Hi, Madison," he said, reaching out and giving her a firm handshake.

"Hi." She smiled and sized him up—just as she was sure he had. She had noticed the two-way mirrors in the training room when she and Jimmy had been fighting.

Troy Carter was, like Jimmy, tall and extremely well built. Whereas Jimmy's Italian good looks and New York accent made him seem like an "ordinary guy," Troy looked former military to Madison. He had close-cropped hair, a soft wheat color, and gray eyes, and his jaw was square. He wore khakis and a golf shirt. His bearing though, his posture, was anything but relaxed. He stood ramrod straight, and she noticed how his eyes moved from one corner of the room to the other, as if he was always on his guard, assessing his surroundings. They were completely safe in the conference room, she knew, but she guessed that because of his background, he had ingrained habits.

"Sit down," he said, sweeping his hand to a chair.

"Thanks." She sat and watched as he opened a case file and sat down to her left—even seated he was stiff.

"After your attack, we sped everything up, Madison. Ordinarily, we'd still be training a month from now, but if your life is in jeopardy, we surmise you're not the only one. On the one hand, we're extremely fortunate. You had a background, frankly, we'd kill for, if you'll pardon the expression. Harvard, MBA from Wharton, multiple languages, fluency especially in French, given your mother's from Paris. And then this little oddity of having been trained by Frank Killian and his boys."

"You know Frank?"

Troy looked up at her. "There's no one in this business who doesn't. But only someone like your father could afford him. Most people only hire Frank and his people to guard them—he's had teams guarding everyone from Shaq to Brad Pitt after his separation, to a few Middle Eastern members of various royal families. The former Shah of Iran's family. But your father is nothing if not controlling."

Madison smiled and nodded.

"For your father, it wasn't enough to have guards. He wanted you to be able to handle any situation that might arise. To keep your wits about you. My understanding is they even put you through three different mock-kidnapping scenarios, and you came through them all with flying colors."

"You're certainly thorough."

"That's my job." He shifted some papers around. "Anyway, Madison, because of this acceleration, I'm going to be with you pretty closely, just to be sure you're ready. In fact, as of Wednesday, I'll be working at Pruitt & Pruitt in the management-training program—real-estate division, of course. You'll be seeing quite a lot of me as an assistant."

"How did you manage that? I mean, Claire was just…well, this is the weekend and this is all, as you said, lightning fast."

"We've been planning this for some time, actually, just hadn't counted on you being part of it."

"I don't understand."

"Madison, I'm about to tell you a few things that are going to be really startling, so brace yourself."

"I don't know how it could be worse than the last couple of days."

"Madison," he sighed, "Claire was working with us already."

"What? She's not a Gotham Rose—wasn't a Gotham Rose."

"I didn't mean that. My fault for not being more clear. I meant she was working with the FBI. She was a whistle-blower, Madison. She was gathering evidence that Pruitt & Pruitt was money laundering for the mob. More specifically, that Pruitt & Pruitt was laundering vast amounts of drug money and that the mob was investing in some of your holdings. We even wondered if it might have ties with the Duke."

"That's the most ludicrous thing I've ever heard of. We're a corporation. We're not some cover for illegal elements of society. We don't even *know* mobsters. And who's the Duke?"

"Someone we've been after a long time. We think he's got his hand in nearly everything—prostitution, money laundering, drugs. And we're convinced he's someone in your social sphere."

"That's absurd."

"Might seem so…but Claire was onto something. She had files and banking papers to prove it."

"But…" Madison looked down at the table, steeling herself for these new revelations. "I had nothing to do with it. And my father…I mean, I was so angry with them, but I believe he loved her. So does this mean she was planning on turning against him?"

"We don't know. She was supposed to meet her contact in the agency the night she was killed. She didn't show up at the meeting point and instead turned up dead in the warehouse."

"Who was her contact?"

Troy looked her directly in the eye. "Me."

"And you had no idea what she was going to say? What she had found as far as proof?"

He shook his head. "She only said it was irrefutable. That Pruitt & Pruitt was into some stuff that would make the Enron boys look like Boy Scouts. She was scared. Terrified, actually."

"Did she implicate my father?"

He shook his head. "She wouldn't say on the telephone. She was getting nervous, jumpy. That's when I secured a job in the management-training program."

"So I'm supposed to find out what my own company is into."

He nodded solemnly. "Even if that means it goes right to the top."

"It won't," Madison said. But now, even she was starting to have doubts. She felt as if she had entered a hall of mirrors—and nothing in her world was what it once seemed.

Chapter 5

There was no use in hiding forever. When Monday morning came, Madison went to the office. The photographers had eased off quite a bit, but around the office some people were crying. A few, who'd been away for the weekend, hadn't even heard until they arrived for work.

As she walked through the impressive executive-level offices at Pruitt & Pruitt, she noticed how both she and her father were looked at more intently than usual. Though Madison, at first, had been scrutinized closely right after college when she started working, after a while, people got used to her being "the big guy's daughter." When her colleagues saw she was a superstar, when they saw she was in the office by six forty-five in the morning and was usually the last to leave—sometimes at ten or eleven at night—they stopped thinking of it as nepotism and started thinking of her as the future leader of their company. After a while, Madison had relaxed and no longer felt as if she was in a fishbowl—until now.

Her father called her into his office. The two of them had corner suites in opposite corners of the top floor. His was furnished to impress with a desk bigger than some conference tables, and floor-to-ceiling windows behind him revealed the skyline—his skyline. One of Pruitt's towers dominated the center of his view.

After Madison shut the door, he started into her.

"You're attacked in your own apartment, and then I can't get ahold of you for two days? That's just unprofessional, Madison. You've got to hold yourself together. And that includes in here. Everyone's watching us to see how we handle the situation. You need to stay focused and professional every minute of the day. Pulling a disappearing act is childish."

"Professional?" Madison arched an eyebrow. "You want me to remain professional? I'm sure everyone thought it was professional when you started sleeping with in-house counsel—a woman your daughter's age. Oh, no, wait, not just your daughter's age but her best friend."

She saw him clench his jaw.

"That was uncalled for."

"Hmmph," she snorted. "There was so much uncalled for in your relationship, I don't know where to start. And now she's gone."

Jack Pruitt stared at his daughter—glared at her was more like it. And she gave it right back at him—which she'd been doing since she was a precocious kid off to nursery school, who insisted on not holding hands. But then, he did something completely uncharacteristic. He put his palms to his face, and his voice grew hoarse with emotion, "Maddie, I swear to you, we never meant to hurt you. And now, I feel like my world is shattered."

It took a few seconds, but Madison softened. "Oh, Dad…I'm sorry. I miss her, too. This is all just like a bad dream."

"Her parents are having her cremated. And they refuse to let me attend the memorial service. They're taking her home to Boston. They never approved of us. Worse, everyone's looking at me, as if I could have harmed her. I couldn't have hurt a hair on her head, Maddie. You have to believe me."

"I do," Madison said softly.

"I'm sure our stock is also going to take a tumble. If this case doesn't get solved soon, if they don't bring her killer to justice, I have no doubt the board of directors will ask me to pull a Martha Stewart. They'll keep me as a figurehead, but install a new CEO."

"Well…it would be temporary, even if they did that. But I don't think it's necessary."

"If it ever becomes necessary, you better be named CEO."

"What about Uncle Bing?"

"Eh…you know, he's great, but he's not as involved in the day-to-day as you are."

Madison nodded. "All right, Dad. Listen, I have a negotiation for the new hotel in the Meatpacking District. I've got to get going. You hang in there."

"I will. Look, while Marcus tries to figure out that security breach on your apartment, I thought of having Frank Killian come in and act as your personal bodyguard."

"No!" Madison said a little too hastily.

"Why? Your safety should be the most important thing, Maddie. Think of Claire. We still have no idea who killed her—or why. And you seem to be the next target."

"No, Dad," Maddie said, more measured, calmer. "I just meant that I have Charlie to drive me any-place. Marcus has been posting an extra guy outside my apartment at night. I'll be fine."

"All right," he said reluctantly. "But we'll play it by ear."

Maddie nodded and left the office. What she hadn't said was that Frank Killian would make her undercover work impossible. There'd be no way she could fool him, slip away when she needed to, nothing. Charlie…well, he was devoted, but she still had her own life. Killian was the type of security profes-sional who didn't even let her use the restroom alone.

Walking briskly back to her office, she soon got lost in her day, racing from meeting to meeting. Next thing she knew, her watch read two o'clock. She hadn't taken a lunch break, and her head was pound-ing. On top of that, it was time to head to Harlem. Her charity, the Harlem Charter School for Excel-lence, was expecting her.

Maddie changed in the private bathroom off her office. The bathroom was equipped with a shower stall big enough for five people, a whirlpool tub and an immense walk-in closet, none of which she ever used, except the closet. She wasn't a clotheshorse. Not in the traditional sense. In fact, she employed a personal shopper named Vanessa Guzman, who basically stocked both her personal and professional wardrobe so Maddie didn't have to shop. She was too impatient to waste her time—another trait she'd inherited from her father.

Still, she liked designer clothes, sunglasses, shoes and bags—and she liked to dress in an unfussy, clean, elegant way that recalled a timelessness. She liked showcasing new designers when she had a charity ball or holiday party. Ashley Thompson had showcased her clothes choices in *Chic*—a photo essay on "young heiresses." According to Tallulah James, a young designer who'd branched out on her own after apprenticing with Richard Tyler, after Madison appeared in *Chic* in the infamous "Hepburn" dress, a little black number that brought to mind a sexier "Breakfast at Tiffany's," Tallulah received enough orders to put her firm in the black—after one season—which was unheard of.

In her dressing room, Maddie shed her work clothes, surveying herself in the three-way mirror. The bruises from both her attack and Jimmy Valentine's training showed when she was naked. She had one bruise on her thigh that had turned an eggplant color. Still, Maddie was proud of her body—taut, busty yet athletic—she knew she looked good. Her abdomen was completely flat, her upper arms toned.

She dressed in a black Donna Karan bodysuit and black jeans. Then she donned a pair of black half boots, pulling the leg of her pants over them, creating a lean silhouette. She put on a black blazer, twisted her blond hair into a loose chignon and touched up her makeup. She added a green scarf around her neck that instantly emphasized her eyes. She scrutinized herself extra carefully.

Maddie tried to kid herself, but then again, she was a no-nonsense person. The truth was she was excited to see John Hernandez.

Exiting the office, she told her administrative assistant she'd be gone for the rest of the day.

"I have my cell phone, though. If Ryan Greene calls, have him call me. That jerk is trying to steal the Aberdeen building right out from under me."

Her assistant, Carla, smiled. "I swear he does that just to get to you."

Maddie smiled. "I think he does. But he knows damn well who he's messing with."

She left the office and then walked ten blocks to the train station, grabbing a subway car bound for Harlem. She could have had Charlie drive her but she always took the train, not wanting to call attention to herself among the children at the school. There, she wanted to be an ordinary volunteer.

The Harlem Charter School for Excellence was the charity she chose for her work with the Gotham Roses when she joined a year ago. She had raised considerable funds for it over the year or so of her time with the Roses. But it was the gift of her time that meant the most to her. Renee always insisted that the Roses spend time—not just money—with their chosen charities. "It's only by pruning ourselves, tending to our inner qualities of compassion, that we can really bloom," was one of her sayings.

At the charter school, which was also supported by very large donations from the Pruitt Family Trust, she went by Madison Taylor. Only the principal knew her true identity. So she was able to show up once a week on Mondays, cutting short her day even though she usually returned to the office to work until the wee hours, to be a homework tutor with John Hernandez's students, and she was able to do so without everyone thinking of her as the spoiled heiress "slumming it." That wasn't who she was or what she was about, but she wanted to be taken at face value.

Unexpectedly, over time, her friendship with the dark-haired young teacher grew until she found herself uncharacteristically with sweaty palms as she walked into John's class each week. This week was no different.

"Here's our homework angel," John said. "Class, say hi to Ms. Taylor."

The classroom full of sixth-graders gave her big smiles and a chorus of hellos. John held her gaze for a few seconds and smiled. Her stomach flip-flopped.

"Hi, everyone," Madison said. "Hello, Mr. Hernandez," she added with a playful tone to her voice.

She left her blazer on but put her purse in his file cabinet and immediately went to the computer-lab area to start helping the kids who were gathered there. She knew all of their names and most of their stories. And her heart both broke and soared for each one.

To be accepted to the charter school, each student had to sign a contract swearing off gangs, drugs and alcohol. They had to commit to two-hour homework sessions four days a week, and to achieving a B average or better—or be put on academic probation. Ideally, John had told her, the parents and family— or grandparents or involved adults—would also commit to the charter school's principles. But that wasn't always the case. Still, these kids made Maddie proud every week.

She leaned over the shoulder of Anna Williams, a favorite student of hers, and checked over her work.

"Great job, sweetie."

Anna beamed. She had high hopes to be a lawyer, and like all the kids in John Hernandez's class, an "anonymous" donor had agreed to fund a college education at a state university for anyone who maintained a B average or better all through high school. Maddie was secretly thrilled to think that someday, perhaps Anna, who was being raised by a very elderly great-grandmother in a wheelchair, might find herself an attorney for Pruitt & Pruitt.

But it was John Hernandez himself who intrigued Madison the most. Little by little he had shared his story. A crack-addict mother, a father shot dead in a drive-by shooting, little John Hernandez was raised by a grandmother who adored him. Even so, he found himself in a gang at ten for protection. He was shot not once, but on two separate occasions, in drive-bys, and he was stabbed in the chest during a fight over turf, the blade narrowly missing his heart.

Lying in a hospital bed in intensive care after being stabbed, he had told Madison that he had been "visited" by the spirit of his father while in a morphine haze, lingering in a netherworld between life and death. John, the most honest person Madison had ever met, had told her his father informed him he would be dead soon if he didn't change his path. Then his father's spirit, John said, laid hands on him and cured him. When John came to hours later, he discovered he had "died" for a full two minutes, only to be paddled and brought back by the trauma team. His young heart had apparently stopped beating and the doctors found a clot they had missed.

John, nearly sixteen, returned to his grandmother's apartment a changed young man. He left the gang, got a job sweeping a Harlem store for minimum wage and worked his ass off to graduate high school on time. Eventually, he started college, applied for grants and got better and better jobs, his disarming good looks and smile winning him fans wherever he went. He had jet-black hair that he wore just a touch long, letting it curl at his collar. His cocoa-colored skin was smooth, and his eyes were so dark you couldn't see his pupils in the black sea of his irises. Full lips, a strong nose and high cheekbones completed his look. Then there was his body, which Maddie decided was perfect, right down to the cross tattoo on his huge left biceps, which she'd spied once when he wore a polo shirt.

Eventually, John Hernandez worked his way up

from the mailroom to a clerical position at Wade and Gonzalez, Attorneys-at-Law. Hector Gonzalez, a partner there, was impressed at the drive John had and mentored him, helping to put John through college with a loan with generous payback terms. Gonzalez always assumed John would perhaps become an attorney, but when he instead went back into his community to make a difference, Gonzalez couldn't argue with him—and admired his commitment.

All Maddie knew was when, at the end of each Monday, he climbed on his Harley and drove away, she felt something inside that Ryan Greene and the other men who could discuss the bull or bear market, the fluctuation of the dollar and the impact of the Pacific Rim's downturned economy on the American economy just didn't do for her. She'd return to the office to work—often until midnight—but uncharacteristically her mind would often wander and replay each word of their conversations.

Maddie and John spent all afternoon with the kids. Every once in a while, he would come over to her and lean over the same student, his shoulder touching hers or his hand leaning on hers as they both held on to the back of the student's chair. The kids would occasionally exchange giggles. Mr. Hernandez's crush on Ms. Taylor was getting harder and harder to hide.

After they had sent the last student home, straightened the desks, shut down all the computers and tidied the room, John said, "Maddie, you're an angel, you really are. You never say why you do this, really, but I'm just grateful you make it here each Monday. I couldn't do this without you. One of me…twenty-five of them. Not a great ratio." He laughed, pulling on a leather jacket. "Um…want to go for a drink?…I mean…I'm sorry. I don't even know if you have plans. Or a boyfriend." He looked at her intently.

"Drinks would be great." *Finally,* she thought. Okay the timing wasn't perfect, but she'd felt something between them for months.

He broke out into an easy grin. "I know the best Tex-Mex place about five blocks from here. Margaritas sound okay?"

"They sound better than okay." Hell, she needed a respite from this last week.

"I was hoping you'd say yes," he said sheepishly, pulling a spare helmet out of his storage closet. "I didn't want to assume, but I brought a helmet. Mind if we take my ride?"

She shook her head and reached up into her hair and pulled out the bobby pins holding her chignon in place. Her hair fell to about three inches below her shoulders. She ran her fingers through it and thought she heard him sigh—a good kind of sigh.

They walked out to the faculty parking lot, climbed on his bike and headed the few blocks to the Tex-Mex place called Tequila Sunrise. Riding there, her teeth chattered a bit, but she wasn't sure if it was from the cold, the vibrations of the Harley, or from gripping him tightly, her hands on his taut stomach, her thighs against his thighs.

She could tell he was a bit of a daredevil—and he liked speed as much as she did. The motorcycle weaved in and out of traffic, the wind whipping her face, and she quickly learned to lean when he leaned, and to become one with the bike—and the driver.

Over drinks, she was amazed at how easily they laughed and talked. She was able to keep steering the conversation to the world at large and away from anything too personal. If he asked her something, like, "What are your parents like?" she didn't lie, but she did commit the sin of omission.

"Oh…they divorced when I was about twelve. It was very bitter. I shuttled between their apartments."

Of course, she left out, "You might have read all the gory details on the front page of the papers. Including how my monthly child support was more than the average teacher's yearly salary." She wasn't ashamed of her wealth—heaven knows she now worked hard enough for it—as did her father—and gave enough of it away. But she feared John would be intimidated by her background, and until he got to know her better, she felt it best to keep him a little in the dark. The photo the newspapers sometimes used was so formal, it barely looked like her—and she didn't tell him her last name was Pruitt. She was simply Madison Taylor.

After drinks, he asked if he could drive her all the way home.

"Oh…no. That's all right, really. I was going to take the subway home."

"At this hour? Not safe, Maddie."

"I'll be fine."

"At least let me hail you a cab and give you cab fare."

"No…really. I ride the subways all the time."

John had signaled the waitress for the bill and paid it.

"I won't take no for an answer."

"How about a compromise? I'll take a cab, but I'll pay for it. You already got drinks."

He hesitated but finally nodded.

Outside the restaurant, they walked back to his Harley.

"It's a beautiful motorcycle." It was—black and lots of chrome.

"It's impractical in the city in a lot of ways, but I love to take it upstate, riding in the mountains. Maybe I can take you some Sunday."

"I'd like that."

"Maddie?"

"Hmm?"

"What would you say to dinner on Friday?"

Friday was actually a board meeting, and she knew she'd be working even later than usual at the office. Plus, she wasn't quite sure how to juggle undercover work with regular work—with volunteering and now a date.

"Um…I have to work late. How about Saturday?"

"Great."

They looked at each other, an awkward moment passing between them. Then John leaned forward and kissed her on the lips. Next thing Maddie knew, she was kissing him back, hungrily. The months and months of exchanged glances and brushing up against each other culminated like an explosion. He had his hands in her hair, gripping her to him, almost making her wince—she was still so bruised from her ordeal.

She bit at his lip sexily, eliciting a moan from him.

"Maddie…" he breathed. "I've thought about this for a long time."

"Me, too," she murmured.

"I've been through so much in my life…and I've kept to myself for so long. I live like a hermit, just…keeping to my mission with the kids, telling myself the right girl is out there somewhere, but not to focus on it. But man…I ache for you."

Maddie felt her legs buckle a tiny bit. *Great,* she mused. *I can take down a two-hundred-twenty-five-pound CIA agent but this guy gets me knock-kneed and tongue-tied.*

"I haven't been with anyone in a long time either, John. I'm married to my job."

This was true. God, Maddie thought, it had been eight months since her last lover, and that had been a disaster. The guy had been too competitive and her greater success was more than he could handle.

"I don't even know what you do exactly."

"Real estate. I try to put together land and development deals. It's really boring, John."

Okay, so it was a little white lie.

"Can I pick you up Saturday? You can't come all the way here. We'll go out in your neck of the woods. Give me your address, and I'll come get you."

"My apartment is undergoing renovation. Why

don't we meet here? I liked it. And it looked like a nice dinner menu."

"You sure? It's not too fancy."

"I'm more interested in you than being taken to some ridiculously overpriced place." *Where I might run into Rubi Cho anyway!*

"All right, angel eyes." He kissed her again, and they stood on the street holding each other for a few minutes. Then he hailed her a cab.

After he had shut the door and the cab pulled away, Maddie gave the driver her address. She was still out of breath and turned on. Then her cooler head prevailed. She pulled out her cell phone. She'd had seventeen calls. She started returning them, and then, rather than going home after all, she told the driver to drop her off at the office. It was time for a pot of coffee and a very late night.

Chapter 6

The office was quiet. Of course, there was plenty of security to get inside the building, let alone the elevator. Still though ordinarily she loved the quiet, tonight it gave her the creeps. She walked silent halls, only the distant whirring of the cleaning crews vacuuming providing any noise.

A few lights in cubicles told her some staff remained. Madison sort of wished chatty Mike Kelly was still at work—he was the department's one-man entertainment unit. But he was in L.A. on business. She'd feel a lot better when Troy officially started on Wednesday.

Maddie settled into her office. She picked up her telephone. Forty-nine voice mails. Forty-nine! She decided voice- and e-mail were the bane of her existence. She began listening. There was a sweet message from Ryan Greene extending his condolences on Claire. Two messages from Claire's mother saying she wanted Madison to have a few of Claire's things. And a message from Charlie checking on her. One from Marcus—same thing. Knowing them, they'd keep calling until she checked in, so she called each of them and said she was working late and would be fine.

She worked for an hour, barely glancing up. Then, after a while, she felt this nagging idea. Who was going to clean out Claire's office?

She rose from her desk and crept down the hall. Feeling guilty for sneaking around, she then berated herself internally. *You head this company, Madison. Get a grip. You owe it to your shareholders to go look around.*

Madison walked more purposefully through the empty hallways to the elevators and took an elevator two flights down to the legal department. She walked to Claire's office, trembling for a minute at the sight of her friend's name on the brass plaque. Maddie still couldn't believe she was gone.

She opened the door and turned on the lights.

Claire's office was a reflection of who she'd been. She collected Steuben-glass pieces, which she displayed in a glass cabinet in the corner of her office. On the walls hung reproductions of Degas paintings—Claire had been a ballerina, training for years until a knee injury forced her to rethink her plans for college and life.

Madison felt as if she was walking into a shrine. She walked around the office, remembering lunches when they sat at Claire's conference table and ate delivered sushi or delectable pastas from one of their favorite restaurants. Whether poring over real-estate contracts or laughing over a rare night together on the town, they could read each other's thoughts— more like sisters than friends.

She strode over to Claire's file cabinets. They were locked, of course. She knew the police had poked around and tried to seize Claire's laptop—but Pruitt's lawyers had given them a tough time and sent them packing with instructions to return with warrants. Moving to Claire's desk, it was also locked, but Maddie knew she kept the key in a Steuben bowl in the cabinet. She found it, opened the desk, and in turn found the key to the filing cabinets. Everything looked in order—and in truth, Maddie had no idea what she was really looking for.

In the second-to-last file cabinet, though, she found something peculiar. Every other cabinet was stuffed to the brim with papers. This one was fairly full, but one file marked "WATERSIDE TOWERS/FINANCING" was empty. Not so much as a shred of paper.

Maddie looked at the file folder in back of the empty one, and the one in front of it, in case the paperwork was just misfiled, but there was no sign of it. Maddie decided to ask Claire's paralegal about it the next day—Waterside Towers would one day stand on the site of the old warehouse where Claire's body had been found.

Shutting the file-cabinet drawer, Maddie heard someone in the hallway, heavy footfalls. Heart beating wildly, she looked around and quickly stepped into Claire's private bathroom, shutting the door except for a sliver.

From the darkened bathroom, Maddie watched in horror as her father strode into the room. He had a look of irritation on his face and made a beeline for the cabinet with the missing file. When he discovered the Waterfront Towers file missing, he cursed under his breath. And when he stood, he kicked the drawer for good measure, and then strode out of the office, turning off the lights as he left.

Madison shrunk back from the door and sat down on the ceramic-tiled steps leading into the tub. Putting her head down onto her knees, she squeezed her eyes shut. Now what? She had told Troy and Renee that she was absolutely convinced of her father's innocence. Yet Renee had told her, the day she arrived to enlist in the undercover agency, that her allegiance had to be to the truth, first and foremost. Maddie had told her that she understood—that she was committed to finding out the truth, not just on this case, but on future cases as well.

But what if the truth all led to one conclusion? And what if that conclusion destroyed not only the corporation she was dedicated to, but her relationship with her father? She was starting to wonder if being an undercover agent would carry with it a price tag, for all her wealth, that she was unable or unwilling to pay.

After seeing her father in Claire's office, Madison decided a trip to Waterside Towers was in order. Tonight—even if it was eleven o'clock.

Because everything about her undercover work had been expedited, and because she had always had a conceal-and-carry permit, she had been issued a Glock, which she hadn't felt necessary to wear.

When she arrived at work that morning, she had locked it in her lower-desk drawer. Now she retrieved it and then left the high-rise offices of Pruitt & Pruitt via the elevator to the parking garage. That was one of the perks of being an executive there. Though there wasn't enough parking for all the employees, those from Senior VP on up got a reserved parking space. Because Madison was, after all, a Pruitt, she got two. She used one to house her second car, an adorable Aston Martin V12 Vanquish painted metallic blue. She climbed behind the wheel, revved up the engine and pulled out of the garage and onto the streets of Manhattan, heading over to the West Side Highway.

She had always loved the West Side Highway. Yes, it had some potholes, but it snaked along the Hudson River, affording a view of the New Jersey side of the water, then, the George Washington Bridge stretched across the Hudson connecting New York City to the other side of New York and, to the south, New Jersey. Maddie loved the sight of the bridge. It was simply majestic at night.

She sped along the highway, and then cut across the GWB, looking often in her rearview mirror. The Aston Martin was fast—and it was small enough that she zipped in and out of lanes. What bothered her was about thirty cars back, so did another car, but because she hadn't seen anyone in the garage, she tried to tell herself it was coincidence.

After she got to the Jersey side, she ended up heading south to the waterfront property. What was going to make the tower site spectacular was not only the view of Manhattan, but its easy accessibility to a high-speed ferry to the city and back again, making the towers a commuter's dream.

She didn't see anyone following her, and about fifteen minutes later, she pulled up to the warehouse. The site was locked with heavy padlocks and chains binding together a chain-link fence. Security lights would come on automatically as she stepped foot on the ground. However, since the warehouse was condemned to be destroyed, and it was abandoned, it was not guarded by an alarm system. The former attack dogs used by the owners Pruitt & Pruitt were purchasing the land from were also now gone.

Maddie took a deep breath. Troy had told her not to go off on her own, but if her father knew something about the Towers and Claire's death, better to find out by herself.

Maddie opened her car door and stepped out. She wasn't even sure what she was looking for. She took off her blazer, checked that her weapon was loaded and stuck it into the holster she had put on. She took her cell phone from her purse, put it on vibrate and walked over to the chain-link fence. It rose up around eight feet, but Madison didn't have a fear of heights. She stuck the toe of her right boot into one of the holes in the fence and began climbing. When she got to the top, she swung a leg over and then carefully climbed down the other side. As she started walking to the warehouse, a German shepherd came out of seemingly nowhere, baring its teeth at her and barking like crazy. So much for the attack dogs being gone.

Maddie knew if she ran, she'd be bitten. And she didn't want to shoot a dog that was just doing its job. Slowly reaching down, she grabbed a two-by-four that was on the ground near her. She moved slowly, calmly, looking the dog in the eye. *Sure,* she thought, *I'd like to see what Jimmy Valentine would say to do here.* Who was she kidding? A real agent would shoot the dog, but the place was abandoned, so she hoped to avoid that unless it became absolutely necessary.

Madison had once read a newspaper story about a woman attacked by a pit bull. In the article, she vaguely recalled something about advice during a dog attack. She kept backing away from the dog.

"Easy there, buddy. Easy…"

When she got to the warehouse, she climbed backward up the fire-escape steps. The dog was still barking and snarling. Then it started lunging at her. Madison thrust the two-by-four forward, wedging it in the dog's jaws. She prayed she could hold the guard dog off until she found an unlocked window or door.

On the second-floor landing, the door was locked, but a window next to it wasn't. In fact, it was shattered.

"It's now or never," Madison said aloud to herself—and the dog.

With all her strength, she shoved downward with the plank, sending the dog careening backward down the metal stairwell, his paws slippery on the metal. Quickly, she climbed through the broken window, careful not to touch a few remaining shards of glass on the sill.

Once inside, she allowed her eyes to adjust to the darkness. She tried to imagine the elegant Claire coming here and navigating all that Maddie had just gone through. That made Maddie wonder—perhaps she hadn't. Maybe whomever Claire was meeting had made sure the gate was unlocked, the dog gone, the doors unlocked. The more Maddie thought about it, the more she was certain that Claire knew who she was meeting and was greeted in a more hospitable fashion.

Maddie wandered the second floor, trying to avoid letting the cold fear in her gut take over. This was where Claire had been killed. Down on the first floor, peering over a metal railing, she could see yellow police tape still strung around a spot on the floor with a dark stain. Maddie felt queasy.

However, any thoughts of queasiness were soon replaced because she could hear the sound of a car's tires crunching on gravel, and the dog began its fevered barking again.

Maddie looked around. Whoever it was would know she was here. They would search the warehouse until they found her. She decided if that was the case, she'd at least be in a good vantage point to take a shot or two at her enemy. And if that enemy turned out to be her father? She'd have to see what the heck he wanted and tell him to come clean. That worry—what she'd find about her father if she came here—had kept her from alerting anyone to her plans. Now she realized how rash she'd acted.

Moving quickly, Maddie opted to hide behind a shipping container. She could peer around the side of it, and she was protected from any returned gunfire.

Whoever was after her, they had the key. From her vantage point, she saw the downstairs door open—a big, wide door, wide enough for a small truck to drive through. Two men came in—neither of whom she had ever seen before.

One made hand gestures, indicating he was going upstairs, and his partner was to look downstairs. They separated, and Maddie readied herself in a shooting stance. Not that she was prepared to kill anyone now or ever.

The guy who was coming upstairs started taunting her in an accent that sounded vaguely Eastern European.

"Come out, Blondie. Come out, come out, wherever you are. We won't hurt you. Much." Then he cackled.

When he reached the upstairs landing he started creeping from side to side in the hall. Moving target, in the dark. Maddie knew as soon as she fired, her position would be revealed. Her heart racing, now her conscience was hoping she could hit him. He had a gun drawn—she had no idea what type it was, but it had a silencer on it, and it looked big. Then she saw a red dot on the wall. *Great,* she thought. *He's got infrared, the better to see me in the dark.*

Maddie lined up a shot as best she could, not wanting to kill, just stop him.

She gently squeezed the trigger, aiming for his thigh—she hit him.

"Son of a fucking bitch! I'm hit!"

Whoever he was, he had stood about six foot three, and now he crumpled like a sack of potatoes, falling to the ground, his gun clattering across the metal floor.

From downstairs, his partner in crime called up to him. "You okay?"

"Shit! I'm bleeding like a stuck pig. Get up here."

Maddie listened, but the guy's partner sure didn't sound as if he was rushing up to his aid. Eventually, the other guy did appear on the landing. He had his gun drawn, too, and then went and stood over his partner. Taking aim, he shot him casually in the head.

Maddie's eyes widened, her adrenaline already pumping after shooing the first guy. Christ, she thought, if he'll do that to his partner, what the hell is he going to do to me?

"Come out, bitch. And I won't kill you."

He started toward her, and she fired off two rounds, both missing wildly. "I've called 911!" she shouted.

He seemed to buy her bluff. He retreated, kicking his partner's body on the way out and muttering something in Russian. She was fluent in French, German and Spanish, but she had a smattering of Russian and Greek. Then she heard the second man running down the metal staircase. She heard another shot and the whimper of the dog. God, who were these guys?

She came out from her hiding spot and then ran outside, avoiding looking at the dead body on the way. She had never been close to a dead body before except at a couple of funerals. Seeing the taillights of their car, she squinted but was unable to get a plate number. She walked across the parking lot and prepared to climb over the fence again.

"Damn them!" All four of her tires were slashed. Her precious Aston Martin. Now she was really mad. Stuck there, with a dead body on the second floor, she realized she had no choice. She took out her cell phone and called Troy. She was an agent for all of a few days and already he was having to come bail her out.

Chapter 7

"Are you out of your mind?"

Troy Carter stared at her. He'd obviously thrown on jeans and a sweatshirt and come straight from bed. His hair was rumpled, and he had major beard stubble.

"No."

He was surveying her car's tires while inside a team of FBI agents processed the dead body.

"Look...I understand that you're used to calling all the shots in your company, and that you are, in some weird, competitive, type-A insane way, cut out for this. But I already feel responsible for what happened to Claire, and I sure as hell don't want to come and find *you* with yellow police tape around your body. So do me a favor and operate just a tiny bit less like a one-woman commando and more like part of a team. Me and you… Here…" He handed her a tiny device that looked like a hearing aid.

"What's this?"

"It's how we keep in touch. It's like a wire. You come to do something like this again, you let me know, for one thing. We do it together. In law enforcement, we have what is called *backup*. It's an amazing concept, backup—I cover your back so you don't end up in a dirty warehouse with two guys wanting to kill you. And then you wear this, which beats a cell phone. We can be in constant contact. And I'll know if something's going down."

"Very James Bond."

"Yeah. Wait till you see some of the gadgets we have for you ladies.… See, you actually get better gadgets than even me."

"How come?"

"Well…we do need you. But we're also aware that most of you come from backgrounds where, no matter how well we train you, there is no way you can be prepared for just how low the bad guys will sink. Not to mention, if something happens to you to blow your cover and word gets out about this undercover team, it's a lot of people's asses—mine included. I don't relish the idea of a desk job in Butt Fuck, Alaska, you know?"

"I hear Butt Fuck can be pretty cold."

"Exactly."

"So…" Maddie said, "who is that guy in there?"

"We don't know yet. The driver's license on him is a fake."

"Big surprise."

"Yeah. And you're *sure* he spoke Russian."

"Absolutely."

"Yeah…the multiple languages. You're a real dummy, I hear." He grinned at her.

"Mm-hmm. Stupid." Away from the training facilities and out in the field, he was downright flirtatious, Maddie thought.

"All right, well, we'll be running his prints, everything. And we'll see what we can come up with. In the meantime, *go home.* And stay home, will ya? Don't ever do anything like this again."

Thinking of witnessing a man get shot in the head, Maddie didn't need convincing. "I won't. But how am I supposed to get home?" She pointed at the Aston Martin.

"Oh, yeah…all right, then, let me talk to some of my guys. I'll drive you."

Troy went and conversed with three agents, then he motioned to her and pointed at a black Acura. "My ride," he said.

"Nice."

"It's no Aston Martin, rich girl." He smiled at her again.

On the way back to Manhattan, Maddie felt she had to make a crucial decision. Tell Troy about her father and the files…or keep her mouth shut. He had given her that speech about teamwork, but she had never relied on anyone before in her life. When she went up against Ryan Greene, for instance, or against steely-eyed negotiators, she was the one at the head of the boardroom table. She called the shots.

But she also knew that, in some ways, this assignment was like *Hansel and Gretel*. Each clue was like a single bread crumb dropped in a dark and eerie forest from which she wasn't sure she'd escape. If she left something out with Troy, maybe evil would overtake them.

"Can I tell you something?"

"Sure," Troy said, hands on the wheel.

"Can I tell you it as my partner? I mean, can we

just sort of keep this between us until I figure it out?"

"What? Figure what out?"

So she told him about Claire's office, the missing files, and how, exactly, she had come to be in the warehouse. She also told him about her father apparently being after the same files himself, and that was why she'd gone to the warehouse alone.

When she was done, she looked over at Troy's profile as they made their way across the George Washington Bridge. He was frowning.

"I wish I knew what Claire had found, Maddie. But it's got something to do with that warehouse, that dead guy, your father, Pruitt & Pruitt, and her murder. I know you believe your father couldn't have had anything to do with her death, but I've been doing this longer than you have, and the sad truth is that people you would never imagine committing a crime will do so when desperate enough."

"But...I don't know. He's brash. He's abrasive sometimes. But he's all about the deal. The blood-letting in the boardroom. The killer deal. Not killing real flesh-and-blood people, let alone someone he supposedly loved."

"There...that."

"What?"

"Supposedly. You added that. Do you know, in your gut, that he really loved her?"

Maddie stared out the window at the lights of Manhattan in the distance as they crossed the bridge. "Honestly? Yeah. I think he did. I was so angry at first, I think I forgot that in the end, it was about how they felt about each other. Even if it hurt me in so many ways."

"Pretty mature of you."

"Yeah, well, I was born mature. My mother *insisted* on mature."

"There's not a whole lot in your file about dear old mom."

"She's complicated. She and I are complicated."

"Eh…me and my father are, too. Former cop. Really hard-core tough guy. His way of showing love was a swift kick to the ass."

"In my case, Mom's an actress. Pretty much retired now. Was considered a famous beauty. When she hit thirty-five, she was already freaking out about aging. By forty, she'd had a lift and her eyes done. And when she and my father got divorced, she was…I have to say, like a rabid she-wolf."

"Nice visual there."

Maddie nodded. "You don't know the half of it.

I mean, she was out for every penny she could get her hands on, in ways that were so petty. Like, she was getting a many-million-dollar settlement, and he was supposed to pay child support—including everything related to my schooling. If she bought me a box of *pens,* she would give him the receipt. She had a bankbook with eight zeros in it, and would charge the man for my pens."

"I'm sorry."

"So am I. You know, I was so ashamed of her—and him. They were so vicious in the divorce. Then, as a single mom, she was worse. She was just husband hunting and expected me to pretty much be all right with a nanny raising me. Dad was building his empire. So, yes, maturity was required."

"You could have ended up one of those spoiled rich girls."

"I'm spoiled." Maddie smiled. "I like the perks that come with never having to look at a price tag. I like my cars, my apartment, my lifestyle. But I'm not a spoiled *brat.* There's a difference. I work for what I have, too. Hard."

"I admire that. You don't have to. Just like you didn't have to accept this assignment."

"I owe it to my father. And to Claire."

"Let's hope we can get the bastard who killed her." Troy said softly.

Maddie nodded, thinking silently. And let's hope that's not my dad.

Chapter 8

Troy Carter, management trainee, started at Pruitt
& Pruitt on Wednesday. The management training
program brought in the brightest candidates and
trained them for nearly a year, which they worked
side by side with a mentor in each major department.
Maddie called human resources and demanded that
Troy spend his first four weeks of training in the real-
estate division. She said she needed the extra manpower, and pretended to show Troy the finer points
of contract negotiation. However, they spent that
first week looking in every conceivable spot for in-

formation on Waterside Towers. They pored over files and looked online at thousands of Word documents and Excel spreadsheets.

By that Friday, Troy came into her office.

"I have those contracts to review, Ms. Pruitt."

"Excellent. Shut the door, Troy."

He did, and for all intents and purposes, they appeared to be two colleagues poring over contracts. With the door shut, he delivered the news. "That dead guy? He's with the Russian mob, who appear to have their fingers in the waterfront deal."

"Why would we get involved with the mob—even unwittingly? We're not desperate for that land. If something looked fishy, we'd walk. I mean, it is harder and harder to put together these big deals, but I don't see my father, Claire, or anyone in this company being dumb enough to climb into bed with anyone that shady."

"The mob doesn't put 'Owned and operated by the Russian mob' on their deeds, Madison. It's all shell companies, so many times removed that tracing them is almost impossible. So maybe those missing files were Claire's proof. The bottom line is we don't know, and until we find them…"

"Well, Claire's paralegal says she has no idea where the files are. I'll have to try Katherine Gould."

"Who's that?"

"She's my uncle Bing's secretary. She used to work for my dad. Bottom line is she is one of the most knowledgeable people in Pruitt & Pruitt. She's helped them build this place—and has a near-photographic memory of every person and file she comes in contact with."

"I love people like that. We have a woman who works in the bureau—Lila. She can remember details on a case from four years ago she only had peripheral contact with."

"Well, I'll talk to Katherine on Monday. I have to go into a board meeting."

"Hey…by the way, did you see today's Rubi Cho column?"

"You read that junk?"

"Oh, come on, admit it. You undercover gals all read her—hell, you're *in* it enough—not so much you but some others of Renee's agents."

"Okay, on occasion, I like my gossip as much as the next person. But no, I didn't see it."

In The Know With Rubi Cho

You know their names: the Pruitts, the Sinclairs, the Daltons, the Whitmans, the Rothschilds. They're the names that dot this column and all society pages, the names of the city's greatest philanthropists and the names of the city's greatest scandals.

Admit it, sweethearts, we all love to read a nice juicy scandal. And a doozy of one is brewing. First Jack Pruitt divorced Chantal Taylor in one of the messiest front-page divorces this city has ever seen. Tales were told of secret lovers and infidelities, not to mention whispers of Taylor's multiple face-lifts (come on…not even a baby's skin is *that* smooth!). But after Taylor left for Paris, the city was on to the next eight-figure divorce-and-custody case.

But this new scandal just may be the juiciest yet. Sources are telling *moi,* Rubi Cho, that the police are, indeed, probing further into the murder of Claire Shipley, and this one has all the makings of front-page tabloid fodder, dear readers. First of all, Claire used to be the best friend of one Madison Taylor-Pruitt, she the Golden Girl of real estate and sometime–arm candy of Ryan Greene. Sure, they deny involvement with each other, but the eternal bachelor has a soft spot for Madison, those same sources tell me.

Once Claire started her love affair with Jack Pruitt, the friendship soured. Until Claire showed up dead in a warehouse *owned* by Pruitt & Pruitt. It all looks a bit fishy to police detectives who are working overtime. And *I* hear that soon, they plan on bringing Pruitt in for formal questioning. Of course, you know he won't arrive without an army of lawyers that'll make the Dream Team look like public-defender hacks. But if the charges stick, could it be that Jack Pruitt will finally be brought down, not by the stock market, or even his own hubris, but by something far darker? Stay posted, kids, because this one ain't going away. But I promise, as soon as I hear it, you'll read it and remain…

In the know…

With Rubi Cho.

Madison rolled her eyes. "You have to take Rubi with a grain of salt."

"Yeah, but the agency is hearing that Briggs, the detective who interviewed you, likes your dad for murder suspect number one. The papers are all hinting at it."

"Well, this is going to make for a very interesting board meeting. If you like being invited to a hanging, you can come sit in."

Hours later, Madison left the magnificent Pruitt boardroom—with its long table, espresso bar and view of Manhattan—with a raging headache. Though the vote had been put off, the board said it was in the best interests of Pruitt & Pruitt's shareholders that if the scandal continued, Jack should indeed "pull a Martha" and step down.

That left Madison and her uncle Bing poised with the support of half the board each for control of the company. Madison had spent her entire career being groomed for the role of her father's successor—but this wasn't the way she wanted to take control.

Chapter 9

The next day, Saturday, Ashley called her.

"Just so you know, Madison, I am *not* Rubi Cho's source."

"Oh, Ash, I wouldn't have thought you were. Most of that was yesterday's news—except for the police angle. But the article was enough to have the board howling at the moon and circling my father like a pack of hyenas."

"It's just awful. Whatever happened to 'innocent until proven guilty'?"

"Come on, remember when that book came out

about my mother? The guy who wrote it picked through our garbage. Our *garbage*."

"The depths people will sink to."

"Exactly. And the people who read that kind of stuff, they don't care about innocence. They just want good dirt."

"What do you say to some martinis tomorrow night? I know the best little intimate bar—the king of the velvet rope keeps out the commoners," Ashley sniffed.

"You are such a snob."

"It girls like us have to be, dah-ling," she said, affecting an accent. "So are we on?"

"Sure, Ash."

"Great. I'll pick you up in *my* limo. Dress to kill, and I'll have a bottle of champagne chilling. We'll forget all about the tabloids—either that or get so drunk we won't care."

"You're crazy."

"Yes, but at least I don't fling my thong around."

Maddie smiled. She hung up her apartment phone just as her cell phone rang. She had her ring tone set to "New York, New York." She loved her town. Looking at the number, she realized it was John Hernandez and her heartbeat quickened a beat or two.

"Hello?"

"Hi, Madison, it's John."

"Hi…" She hoped he wasn't calling to cancel.

"Listen, I don't know how close you are to Central Park, but what would you say to me riding my motorcycle in and meeting you there, and taking a long stroll, then we can still go for Tex-Mex if you want."

"Sounds wonderful. I'll you meet over by the Metropolitan Museum of Art."

"About two o'clock?"

"Perfect."

Maddie hung up and looked out her window. Central Park was her backyard, for God's sake. Originally, she'd told John she was "Maddie Taylor"—an ordinary volunteer—precisely because she wanted to be treated as ordinary. But now, she hated the web of tiny white lies she'd created. All right, maybe not so tiny. She hoped he didn't read the *Wall Street Journal.* She hoped, until the time was just right, she could keep her real name and position at Pruitt & Pruitt a secret.

She felt guilty about her situation, but at the same time, she thought as she turned around and surveyed the art in her apartment, how would John deal with the fact that paintings by Paul Klee and Basquiat hung in her hallway? That she owned whole *buildings?*

* * *

Dressed in a pair of black velvet jeans and a warm emerald-colored cashmere sweater, Maddie waited by the museum steps. The Pruitt Family Trust always gave generously to the arts in Manhattan, and there was a gallery named for her great-grandmother in the museum.

Soon, John came strolling up in the afternoon sun. He wore a black leather jacket, jeans and black boots, and he had a confident stride—not a swagger, but definitely the walk of a man comfortable in his own skin. He smiled as he approached her and then kissed her on the cheek.

"You look like a million bucks," he said.

"Thanks…" If only he knew how true that was. Though technically it was a hundred-million bucks—give or take.

He grabbed her hand as they started strolling down the street toward the park. Madison cast a side-long look at him. He was so different from the men she dated—when she had time. Still, compared to the men she knew, John was so open. He didn't seem interested in playing games. And here, on the street, he was openly affectionate. She was used to men like Parker Whittington III, who wouldn't hold her hand if his life depended on it. She guessed it was from a lifetime of being raised by nannies and distant parents. Madison's mother hated being kissed in public—or private. Her father used to sneak into the nursery, when he was still married to her mother, and give her bedtime kisses if he was home. Otherwise, the only tucking in she got was from Matilda, her old nighttime nanny. Her day nanny had gone on to work for another prominent New York family, but Madison always felt it was to her father's credit that he still kept Matilda on—though her only duty now was tending to a lone Cavalier King Charles spaniel at Jack's country house. Matilda, seventy-two now, spent her days reading and doing needlework, flower arranging, and enjoying her semiretirement. As Madison strolled, she realized there was much more to her father than his ruthless reputation, and she hoped the police would find that out, too.

When John and Madison got to the park, they aimlessly wandered down paths, talking. When they got to the Wolman Skating Rink, Madison stopped still when she spied the Russian from the night at the warehouse—the one who'd shot his partner. He was with a new partner now, a shorter, squat man with a black overcoat. Whereas everyone else seemed focused on their kids, or on people watching, the two men's only focus appeared to be Madison—and now

John. Fear gripped her throat, and Madison leaned into John.

"Where'd you park your motorcycle?"

"Not too far from here…found a spot on the street. Must be my lucky day."

Not if these guys get ahold of us, it won't be, Maddie thought. "I was wondering…what if we changed plans and took that drive upstate? It's a really pretty day."

He looked at her and wrapped an arm around her shoulder. "You going to be warm enough in this sweater? Maybe we should drop by your place and pick up a jacket."

"No, that's okay, really. I'm always warm."

"All right, let's go then. You know, I think I have a sweatshirt in my saddlebag. It won't match your outfit, but for the ride, it'll be fine, if you don't mind, and will give you another layer."

"Great!" Maddie smiled up at him, and he pulled her against him and kissed her on the mouth.

"I just had to do that," he growled.

Despite really preferring to go find a bench and kiss him all afternoon, Maddie knew she had to get them out of the park and out of the city. Now. "Come on," she purred, hoping he would be anxious to get on the motorcycle together.

"All right," he said reluctantly. Arm around her shoulder, he steered her out of the park and toward his bike. Looking over her shoulder, Maddie saw the Russian and his pal following them. The Russian had a square jaw and eyes the color of a pale blue glacier. They were only a few yards back. She quickened her pace, and John instinctively kept step with her.

They reached his motorcycle, and he handed her his sweatshirt—a black one with the Harley insignia on it. *If my peers could see me now,* she mused. She donned the warm sweatshirt and the shiny black helmet he had and climbed on the bike in back of him.

Within minutes, they were roaring through Manhattan. At a couple of lights, she looked over her shoulder. No one appeared to be following her and John, and she felt herself relax and actually enjoy the ride. She assumed that the two mobsters had decided that a scene in broad daylight—when she was with a well-built, tough-looking guy herself—was not in their best interest.

Eventually, they drove up the Palisades Parkway, which snaked up along the Hudson River all the way to Bear Mountain and West Point. The farther north they got, the more traffic there was—which was the opposite of normal—when closer to the city usually meant more traffic. But Madison remembered the morning newscaster rating the day as one of the top choices for fall foliage. She did marvel at the hues of gold and burnished reds. She felt, as they drove on into the mountains, the colder air as it hit her face. She buried her right cheek against John's back. She was amazed at how much just touching him on the motorcycle gave her feelings she frankly had never thought she'd have. She was too controlled, too much like her father, too much a woman who had to play with the big boys and never let them see her break a sweat.

He slowed the Harley as they came to the circle near West Point.

"You cold?" he shouted over the roar of the motorcycle.

"Just a little."

"We'll stop in a little bit for some coffee. I know a roadside diner."

As they completed the circle, she saw John look in his side-view mirrors and felt him stiffen.

"What?" she shouted.

"Some asshole is creeping up on my tail."

Maddie glanced behind them and saw a black Mercedes sedan with black-tinted windows speeding up on them.

John revved the bike and leaned forward a bit. But

the more he sped up, the more the black car kept up with them. "What the hell…" John shouted against the wind.

Maddie instinctively leaned against him, almost as if she willed him to go faster. She could handle the speed.

"Hang on!" he yelled. Suddenly, the motorcycle's full capabilities were on display. John had the bike going ninety-five miles an hour, and he zipped in front of two slower cars, trying to put some distance between them and the Mercedes sedan.

However, Maddie could glimpse the sedan in his side-view mirrors. The driver of the car—and she assumed it was the Russian or his sidekick—had no respect for the law—or safety. The car pulled out into the no-passing lane and gained on them.

John urged the motorcycle faster, and they raced along the winding turns of the upper Palisades Parkway as other cars leisurely drove, taking in the sights of the fall trees in all their glory.

"I have an idea," he yelled back at her.

Maddie gripped him tighter, moving her lips in an involuntary prayer of the Our Father, though she hadn't been to church in years.

John sped along the parkway, slowed slightly, and made a turn into the Bear Mountain Park. He exited the park almost as soon as he entered it, by making a 360-degree turn in the parking lot, leaning the bike way down, almost on its side. Maddie leaned with him, trying to meld their bodies as one so there was no resistance. The sedan spun around, too, and followed them as John drove back the way they had come. Soon they arrived back at the West Point circle, only this time, he headed right toward the West Point campus. Slowing, they arrived at the entry gate, where soldiers manned a sentry post.

West Point, aside from being an officer-training school, was also a huge tourist attraction. It had a beautiful view of the Hudson, not to mention incredible historical significance, and a museum. John paid to park, acting as if they were tourists, after telling the guard on duty they were there to sightsee.

As John pulled the bike onto the campus, Maddie marveled at all the gray-uniformed cadets, walking ramrod straight, eyes forward, cap bills pulled down. John was brilliant, she decided. There was no way, in this political climate, that the two guys in the Mercedes would try anything on the campus. She felt John relax—and so did she.

They found a parking spot and climbed off the bike and removed their helmets.

"Who were those guys?" John asked.

Maddie shrugged. "I don't know. Maybe some random weirdos."

He stared at her. "Maddie…random weirdos in a hundred-fifty-thousand-dollar cars don't decide to run people off the road in broad daylight. Did you get a look at their faces?"

"No. I was too busy holding on for dear life."

"Look, is there something you're not telling me?" His voice was filled with worry.

"Like what?" Maddie opened her eyes wide, feigning innocence.

"I don't know…forget it. Maybe they were just screwing around with me because of the Harley. A testosterone thing. Speaking of…" He pulled her to him and kissed her. "As long as we're here, want to take a walk around?"

She nodded. Anything to get his mind off the motorcycle ride. "First I need to use the ladies' room."

He craned his head, saw some signs, and they made their way to the museum, where she went into the ladies' room while he waited outside. Once she was in a stall, she dialed Troy.

"Agent Carter here."

"Troy, it's Madison…listen, I don't have a lot of time. I was out on a date when the Russian and a stocky pal saw me in Central Park—they were obviously following me. Long story but my date drove me out the city. Then the Russian and his friend nearly ran me—us—off the road."

"You okay?"

"Yeah. Fine. Now."

"Where are you?"

"West Point."

"The military academy?"

"That's the only West Point I know, Troy."

"Sorry…it's just you're way upstate. I'll leave now. These goons still around?"

"No. And I'm actually going to be heading back to the city soon. I'll be fine. I just thought you should know. You told me I should check in with you. You know, after the whole thing at the warehouse."

"You actually listened. I'm shocked, but stay put until I can get there."

"And how will I explain that to my date? Look, I'm going back to the city. I'll check in, I promise. But for now, I'm safe."

Troy didn't respond. After a few seconds, Maddie said, "Hello? You still there?"

"Yeah. I'm weighing whether or not to let you go back on your own or waiting, which has its own risks. All right…you can head back on your own, but check in."

"Okay. I'll talk to you tomorrow." Maddie broke the connection and emerged from the stall. She left the rest room, and her heart skipped a beat when she didn't see John. Then he rounded the corner, carrying two hot chocolates in plastic cups.

She smiled and wrapped her hands around the steaming cup he handed her.

"Warm up…it'll be a cold ride back to the city. I thought, to be safe, we'll cross the Bear Mountain Bridge and head back on the Westchester side of the Hudson."

"You're the pilot." She grinned at him as they left the building, blending in with the crowds of tourists enjoying the fall foliage.

They walked back to the motorcycle, and before they put on their helmets, John asked her, "Are you sure there's not something you want to tell me?"

She nodded.

He looked at her skeptically. "Okay… Listen, instead of that Tex-Mex place, I was thinking of cooking for you. I'm no gourmet, but I make a mean paella."

"Sounds delicious."

"Then hop aboard my magic carpet and off we go."

The ride back to the city was uneventful, but

Maddie kept looking over her shoulder anyway, and John kept glancing in his side-view mirrors. Finally, they reached the outskirts of the city. As they sped along the streets of Harlem, they eventually reached an area that was gentrifying. Buildings were spruced up, townhomes were showing signs of renovation, and small shops and groceries and bakeries were bustling with afternoon activity.

John pulled next to a small town house, and parked his bike in a spot next to the building. Painted on the blacktop was white paint that read Apartment 2B.

They took their helmets, and she followed him into his building, a brownstone divided into two apartments on each floor.

Apartment 2B was a one-bedroom with a large, open living-room area that doubled as a dining area, and a decent-size kitchen. Long, narrow windows with crown molding let in a little afternoon sun onto hardwood floors.

"This is really lovely," Maddie said, looking around. "I like the floors—old-fashioned hard-wood."

"Did 'em myself," John said proudly. "They were here, but under the most god-awful carpet you ever saw. I had to refinish them. I got into this building ages ago when, trust me, you wouldn't even want to walk down the block. I fixed the apartment up, put in the crown molding, did those shelves there. Spruced up my place, and little by little, the neighborhood spruced up, too."

Maddie looked around. His furnishings were eclectic—if she had to put her finger on it, she'd say there was a vague Asian influence mixed with some flea-market finds. On one table sat what looked like a real Tiffany lamp. She walked over and touched it.

"That was my grandmother's."

"It's beautiful."

"What's your apartment like?"

"Oh…you'll see it one day. It's nice. You know… um…a little more traditional. But nice."

She felt herself getting in deeper and deeper with her lies.

"Come on over here, and I'll pour you some wine while I cook."

He uncorked a bottle of cabernet, and Maddie sat on a wicker stool at his breakfast bar and watched him while he carefully prepared dinner.

"Can I help?"

"No. I decided yesterday I would rather cook for you and spend an evening alone together, talking, instead of in a noisy restaurant, so I'm all set. If you want, go turn on the stereo over there. I have it pre-set to some stations. I think the second button is a jazz one. The first is classical. Moving up it gets into rock. One hip-hop."

Maddie climbed down from the stool and turned on the stereo, ultimately choosing the jazz station. She pulled out her cell, text messaged Troy "IM OK," then she went back to watch John as he bus-ied himself in the kitchen.

Funny, she thought, she had grown up with a chef in her home. But he treated the immense kitchen with its restaurant ranges and subzero re-frigerators, and built-in wine coolers, like a restau-rant. Joseph would chase her out of "his" kitchen, and because her mother insisted on a macrobiotic diet—the better to avoid adolescent weight gain, she told Madison—the "poor little rich girl" had never even licked cake batter from beaters. Or watched anyone prepare an entire meal. She tried to imagine Ryan Greene—or any of the men she knew, for that matter—chopping onions or peeling garlic.

Over wine, John told her more about his child-hood, and his first forays into the gang.

"Have you ever really hurt someone?" she asked

him, thinking clearly for the first time of pulling the trigger at the warehouse.

He nodded. "One of the requirements for getting into the gang was you had to commit a mugging. So I did. I was so tired of getting jumped on my way to school. The gangs offered a street family. So I mugged someone—an older guy on his way home from work. He had on a uniform for a gas station. Old guy, like I said. Looked a little frail. But he ended up having a gun. I wrestled him for it…and I hit him on the head."

"Was he okay?"

"Yeah. I mean, I'm sure he had a big welt the next day. But I felt terrible."

"It's hard to picture you doing something like that. When I see you in class, those kids absolutely revere you."

"Well, at the end of the day, it's about making a difference. It's not about how much money you have, or your possessions…"

She thought about being an agent. Would she be able to make a difference so that Claire did not die in vain? That was part of how Renee put it. She had a chance to *do* something.

After an hour or two of simmering, dinner was done. John uncorked a second bottle of wine and lit some candles. While he did that, she helped set the table. On his refrigerator, she noticed pictures of his class—including one of her, front and center on the fridge, leaning in next to Anna as they worked on the computer. She smiled to herself.

Over dinner, they sat and ate, as usual the conversation not lagging. After they finished, he invited her into the living-room area. "When we've digested dinner, I've got a homemade dessert. I made flan yesterday, but I'm too full—unless you're still hungry."

"Not me. Stuffed for right now. But dinner was wonderful."

He refilled her wineglass and sat next to her on the couch, draping an arm around her. She was surprised at how comfortable she felt around him. She was so used to being cautious.

He turned his face to her, his dark eyes full of passion and intensity, and began kissing her neck. He moved his arm from her shoulder to take her face in his hands. Soon, they were kissing ravenously.

Madison had never felt anything that she would describe as raw passion before. Her few boyfriends over the years had been as tightly wound in their careers as she was. They scheduled sex into their

PalmPilots and BlackBerry PDAs and arranged dates after board meetings—often canceling at a moment's notice for business reasons. But this, with John, was a hunger, and they hurriedly undressed each other, moving from the living room to his bedroom, which was cozy and lit by a small night-light.

When he entered her, she was amazed at his strong, hard body, but more than that, she was breathless from the emotions he seemed to project, this intensity that took her breath away. He grabbed at her hair, and she found herself wrapping her fingers in the dark curls at the nape of his neck, moaning in rhythm to the way he made love—because that's how it really felt—to her.

When they were both spent, it still wasn't over—not the way she was used to. They kissed for an hour, maybe more, eventually their passion growing again. And in some ways, Madison Taylor-Pruitt knew she would never again be satisfied with trust-funders again. It was John Hernandez she craved.

After he finally fell asleep, his breath heavy on her shoulder, his arms tightly wound around her, she thought again of the bad guys following her. They were just one of many secrets she now kept from John, and she found she wanted to wake him up and tell him everything, but something held her back. And she hoped, and even prayed a little, that one day John would understand.

Chapter 10

"Slumming?"

She and Ashley were drinking Blue Pearl martinis at the Blue Pearl Club, known for its signature drink. At sixty bucks a pop, the martinis had an ever so slight bluish tinge, almost like an abalone shell, and real pearl dust—edible, Ash explained.

"I'm not slumming."

"Well, you're screwing some hot Latino lover from Harlem, honey, what would you call it?"

"Ashley…give me a break. I've known him a long time through my charity. This has been developing."

Ashley tucked a stray piece of hair behind her ear—where diamond earrings hung from her delicate lobes.

"I once went slumming. It was the summer of my senior year of college, and my boyfriend at the time—you know, the rum-and-whiskey heir I told you about…the one with the big bankbook but the tiny penis—well, he was boring me to no end. Knee deep in some kind of merger. Always at the office. And things in the bedroom weren't exactly rocking my world."

Madison sipped her martini. It was delicious, she'd give Ashley that. "And?"

"*And* my father was whisking me off to Monaco for a little R&R while he handled some kind of business. And I met a Frenchman."

"Since when is a Frenchman slumming it?"

"When he's a croupier, darling. He worked in a casino in Monte Carlo. And he looked absolutely delicious in a tuxedo."

"You're incorrigible."

"You don't know the half of it. As a lover, he spoiled me for eternity, Maddie. Oh, what that man could do in bed. But, after a while, I realized it was somewhat mechanical. You know, like he was such a good lover, it was all about how he could play me like a violin, rather than any real passion. Still…a great summer."

"Well…" Madison mused. "This was real passion. Real."

"So what does he think of the fact you don't blink at dropping sixty bucks on a martini? Or the fact that your great-grandmother used to spend the summers with Eleanor Roosevelt? Or the art collection…?"

Madison blushed.

"What?"

"I haven't told him yet."

"You are kidding me."

"Nope. I kind of wish I was."

Ashley shook her head. "Girlfriend…you are asking for trouble. Because the way you talk about this guy, I think you really care about him. And that's dangerous. Have your boy toy, Madison, but settle down with someone like Ryan. Someone who really gets you. Otherwise you're going to have a mess on your hands, I promise you."

"Give me a break. Look, even when socialites wed 'their own kind,' like you're talking about, it doesn't usually work out. Can you honestly tell me that you would really be satisfied having a boy-toy gardener or whatever on the side while pretending to be happily married in some socially acceptable marriage?"

Ashley had a twinkle in her eye. "Ever notice how my mother always looks so refreshed? Well, trust me, my father is gone on business—with his secretary—about a hundred days of the year. And Mom? She's got a very hot yoga instructor who gives her private lessons right in her home."

"You're horrible, Ash!"

"No, just practical."

The two women soaked up the scene. Madison spotted Tatiana—one of the other Gotham Rose agents. Tatiana walked by her and Ash and winked at Madison.

"What was that?" Ash asked.

Madison shrugged. She decided to head home. Ash volunteered her limo, but Madison wanted to clear her head from the events of the weekend.

She walked the fourteen blocks to her building, every nerve on fire. She kept waiting to run into the Russian. She stayed alert, and felt at her back for the gun she wore. She wondered if she would ever get used to wearing a gun as an agent. She wondered if she would ever get used to being an agent.

She knew though she couldn't see them, Troy and another agent were watching her. She spied a white van and assumed it was them.

At her apartment, the doorman, Jean-Paul, tipped

his cap and opened the heavy glass-and-brass door for her. Stepping into the lobby, the nighttime concierge stopped her.

"Ms. Pruitt?"

"Hmm?"

"A package arrived for you this evening."

"From whom? It's Sunday."

"I know. It was hand delivered. By a chauffeur, by the looks of his uniform."

"Did he say who he was or anything?"

The concierge shook his head. "He just said he was asked to deliver it."

Madison eyed the box suspiciously but took it. Then she went to the elevator. The Sunday elevator operator, Antonio, pressed the button for the penthouse and she rode in silence to the top, staring down at the box in her hands. It wasn't too heavy. And it wasn't ticking. She half smiled to herself. She couldn't believe how her mind was starting to work. She assumed the box wasn't a bomb, but she still found the whole thing curious and couldn't wait to be alone and open it. Then she stopped herself. Maybe it *would* be better if Troy was there.

She called him and he arrived within ten minutes. She let him into her apartment, and he went over to the box with some equipment similar to the wand used at airport security. He declared the box safe, and sliced into it with a sharp kitchen knife.

Madison peered into the box.

Inside was a strange collection of objects that seemed unrelated to one another, and a letter in a white envelope.

With shaking hands, Madison opened the letter and read it aloud to Troy.

Dear Madison,

This box is from Claire. She made me promise that if anything happened to her, I would have it hand delivered to you.

As you know, her father and I never approved of what she was doing at the end. And I know I will never get over her death. I would have some small measure of peace if I knew that the bastard responsible was in prison…but I am as confused as ever over the whole thing. And this box confused me, too. Did she know she was going to be murdered?

Part of me was tempted not to have it delivered. And I wish with all my heart I knew what these things meant. Maybe you do. If you figure it all out, maybe you can call me someday and tell me. I'd like to know what was on her mind in her final week on earth.

Her father and I were always very, very fond of you, Madison. Do keep in touch.

Sharon Shipley

Madison took out the objects one by one and laid them on the table:

A travel brochure from the Caymans

A key

A photo of the Manhattan skyline

Claire's passport

A seashell

And finally, a map of New York and New Jersey.

Maddie opened the map, and there was a tiny red dot of ink on a town she had never heard of. Venetian Lake. In the upper corner of New York near the Canadian border.

"Looks like we'll be taking a road trip," Maddie muttered.

Then she sat down at the table with Troy and tried to figure out just what Claire was trying to say to her from beyond the grave.

Chapter 11

Venetian Lake turned out to be a tiny hamlet—population 282—in upstate New York. In the center of town stood a cannon in tribute to the three young men from Venetian Lake who had been killed in World War II. Aside from the cannon, there was a firehouse, a single grocery store, a pizza parlor, a gas station and a Laundromat.

Maddie drove herself and Troy in her now-repaired Aston Martin into town. She had taken off Monday afternoon. Frankly, she thought, this undercover agenting was going to be tricky. She was in the middle of hostile board meetings, heated negotiations over a hotel in the now uber-trendy Meatpacking District, and a major construction project—and it certainly wasn't like her to tell her assistant that she was going to be out for the remainder of the day. But in this case, she had to find out what secrets lay in this lake town. She and Troy headed off on the open highway, and Maddie was enjoying the escape for the day.

The "lake" in question was more of a very large pond, she decided. She couldn't fathom, for the life of her, how it earned its moniker. But she knew the best way to find out would be to ask at the one place she was sure gossip—albeit masculine gossip—was handed out. The volunteer fire station.

"You sure you haven't been doing this cloak and dagger stuff your whole life?" Troy teased when he realized where they were headed.

She smiled as she pulled the car into the concrete driveway next to the building. The building was brick with a large bell above its garage door. She imagined it occasionally clanging in the night. They went to the front—the immense garage door was open, and two firemen were washing the lone red truck. She could smell spaghetti sauce or something simmering in the firehouse kitchen.

The younger guy with the shaved head—hot enough for a firemen calendar—stood up and wiped his forehead as she and Troy climbed out of the car. "Can I help you?"

"I'm sorry—" she batted her eyes "—we're just plain lost. We were heading to Lake Placid for our honeymoon and got the bright idea to take some back roads and drive through some small towns. And…we ended up here. Starving—and the pizza place looks closed right now. I don't know if there's someplace else to eat."

He grinned at them. "Congratulations. I'm married three years now. There's nothing else around for miles, but you're more than welcome to join us for dinner."

"Is that an invitation?"

The older fireman, silver-haired with a barrel chest and big white beard that made him look like Santa in the off-season, said, "That is, if you don't mind spaghetti and meatballs."

"I'm so famished, I could eat shoe leather," Troy joked.

"Come on then," the younger fireman said. They turned off the hoses they were using to wash the truck. He then dried off his hands on a nearby towel and turned around. "I'm Tommy Malone, and this is Vic Keel."

Maddie smiled at them both and shook their hands. "Madison Taylor," she said, "and my husband, Troy."

They followed the men into the firehouse kitchen. It was homey, with blue-and-white-gingham curtains on the windows of the living area. Madison guessed someone's wife had sewn them.

The firemen set the table, and after stirring the pot a couple of times, Vic came over with four heaping bowls full of spaghetti and topped with huge meatballs and red sauce. Maddie's mouth watered, though she knew there was little chance she'd even come close to finishing hers.

The men dug in heartily, after pouring sodas for each of them, and she cut into one of her meatballs with her fork and tasted it. "This is fantastic! And whoever said men can't cook," she said and smiled playfully.

Troy ate like he'd never been fed before. "Awesome."

"Man, Vic is the best," Tommy said. "Everyone loves when it's his turn to cook. With me, everyone gets hot dogs or chili."

"You know," Madison said, twirling her spaghetti, "this is such a pretty little town—lots of cottages on your lake and so on. Why is it called Venetian Lake, though?"

Tommy looked at Vic. "He's the resident historian."

Vic put down his fork and sipped a Coke. "Well, you see a bunch of cottages, but at one time, there was a big ol' house on the hill in back of the Episcopal church. Some rich guy aimed to make this a summer playground for the wealthy. He bought up all the land and wanted it to be like a small European town, or someplace classy. Picked Nice as a name—though of course everyone in these parts pronounced it *nice,* not *niece* as in the popular city on the French Riviera. He owned the damn town lock, stock, and barrel. He could have named it whatever he damn well pleased."

Maddie smiled. Then she felt a small chill pass over her. "Nice...that sounds so familiar. I mean other than the French Riviera." It couldn't be.

"Sure. It was kind of famous. 'Cause a not-so-nice thing happened here. 'Course, you're way too young to remember, but there was a kidnapping here—as famous as the Lindbergh case—at the time at least."

"Sure," Madison whispered. "The Pruitt baby."

"Yup. But see, after that poor child turned up dead, God, fifty-five years ago or so, Mrs. Pruitt had a breakdown. So her husband sold the town to one of his best friends, a guy by the name of Rockefeller. He demolished the old house and planned on putting in some new, fancy modern house, designed by Frank Lloyd Wright. But then his wife decided she didn't like the socializing here—as in there was no socializing. So they in turn sold the town. When they did, they sold it to a developer who put in all these cottages, and the developer didn't want people remembering the kidnapping. So he renamed the town Venetian Lake. Now, no one remembers its old name—and most especially, no one remembers what happened here."

"Since then, I don't even think there's been a single homicide," said Tommy.

"Amazing," Madison said, exchanging meaningful looks with Troy. She knew the baby died in *Nice*. How had Claire come to discover the change of name? And what did this place's tragic history have to do with the present day?

"Yeah. And if you go by the church, there's the mausoleum for that poor family. But only the baby is in it."

"Hmm." Madison nodded. "You ever know them?"

"Nah. Been too long."

"Does anyone ever come to visit the baby's grave?"

Madison herself had never been there, and the topic was taboo in the family.

"Nope. Nobody. Sometimes the minister's wife puts fresh flowers there. She tends to the cemetery a bit. Lovely woman."

Troy asked, "Any curiosity seekers come here?"

Vic shook his head. "Wait, though," he furrowed his brow. "I remember one woman. Said she was a friend of the family's. This was a while back. Pretty gal. Dark haired. But, that was it."

Convinced there was no more to be told, Maddie said, "Tell us more about the fire station." She had learned, from her years in business, that the best way to avoid talking about herself was to ask people about themselves—most were only too happy to oblige. However, she found the firemen modest and patriotic. They regaled her and Troy with tales from their small town, then walked the two outside to her car and waved goodbye. Madison made a mental note to send an anonymous donation to the firehouse.

Madison and Troy pulled away and drove around the lake, glimpsing the dark blue water through the trees. Maddie spotted the white spire of the church she thought the firemen had referred to, and she drove in that direction, eventually finding the Episcopal church and its cemetery. Behind the church, up on the hill where, she now knew, the family home once rose, stood three smaller homes with white picket fences and sweeping lawns. Fall leaves blanketed the grass, and in the yard of one house, a golden retriever bounded, chasing falling leaves.

She parked the car next to the cemetery. Troy climbed out and said, "I'm going to go check out the church, see if maybe the minister or his wife is there."

"Okay, I'm going to find the baby's grave."

Maddie walked through the wrought-iron gates—unlocked and open—and began strolling down the rows of graves. Most were neat and tidy, but near the edge of the cemetery, along a row of trees, the graves were more haphazard and dated from the turn of the century. The dates were nearly faded in the stone by years of weathering and wear.

She saw, also near several trees, a very large mausoleum. Maddie walked over to it, her feet crunching in the dead autumn leaves.

She read the inscription carved in white marble: Angels and Saints of the Pruitt Family. An enormous wrought-iron gate, about fourteen feet high, stood in front. She pressed on the gate, and it opened easily. Five marble steps led down into a tunnel-like entrance to the mausoleum. Maddie walked down, and allowed her eyes to adjust to the darkness. Inside the mausoleum it was about ten or fifteen degrees cooler than the already-brisk fall air, and she shivered slightly. In the pale light that seeped in from the entrance, she saw a single tile in a wall engraved: William Charles Pruitt III, beloved son and brother, 1947–1948. Maddie's eyes welled for a moment, thinking of how her poor grandmother must have been crushed by the crime. She ran her fingertips along the engraved marble, its feel icy to the touch. She shook her head ever so slightly. What could this poor baby's death have to do with Claire's murder? Little William was murdered, too. But how could the two murders many decades apart have anything to do with each other?

Maddie was completely puzzled. And, lost in her own private thoughts, she never heard the attacker sneak up on her and hit her over the head with a metal pipe. She only saw blackness as she collapsed to the ground.

Chapter 12

Hours later, her teeth chattering, Maddie woke up. At least she thought it was hours later. It could have been ten minutes, it could have been a day. All she knew was it was pitch-black. And she was cold, colder than she had ever been. And she had a splitting headache. She could hear two men whispering outside, and she struggled to sit up, the movement sending shattering waves of pain through her temples and neck.

Quietly, she felt at her back. Her gun was still there. No one knew she was an agent, and whoever was after her would have no idea she was carrying a weapon. She guessed they thought she was just a curious heiress looking into her past, or into whatever mystery Claire had stumbled on. Was this how Claire had met her death? Was some of it from snooping into a long-forgotten murder? And where was Troy?

Maddie quietly pulled herself into a standing position and crept closer to the opening to outside. She pulled her gun from its holster. In the darkness, she saw one man's face slightly illuminated by the glow from a cigarette. She didn't recognize him. She overheard the other man say, "We wait for the word. I think just getting rid of her fits with the plan anyway."

She didn't recognize his voice or his profile in the dark, either. But she was scared. *Getting rid of her?*

The two men stood close together, talking in low voices.

"She'll be out cold for a week. Or dead," the taller one said, laughing a little.

Maddie knew she had to get them both. If she left one standing, she was as good as dead.

Taking her gun, she aimed at the taller one and fired, hitting him between the shoulder and his chest, and spinning him around. He fell to the ground with a weird sort of grunt, and the other one drew his gun, facing her in the darkness. "What the fuck!" he shouted.

He aimed wildly in the dark, missing her, and she heard the bullet echo inside the mausoleum. He fired again, and she ducked, then took aim from a crouching position and fired. She hit him in the leg, but she guessed it was just a grazing bullet, because though he cursed, he was still standing. She took advantage of his pain, though, to slip out of the mausoleum and dash out into the cemetery.

Over her head another bullet whistled, and she heard him on his cell phone shouting he had "trouble."

She dived behind a large headstone. If she called 911 or local police, she feared some inexperienced country cop would get killed. She was convinced she had to escape herself—and find Troy. Fear coursed through her. What if they had killed Troy? She was on her own and would have to think and operate like an agent until she found her partner. Screw these bastards. She had been underestimated in the boardroom before, and she didn't like it. And now these guys had no idea who they were messing with.

From behind the headstone, she fired at her assailant. She missed, and he fired back.

The moon was just a sliver, and it gave off little light. She squinted and dove for a different headstone, one a few yards down and closer to where she'd parked her car. She scrunched down. She only had a single clip in her weapon. Scaring him off wasn't an option. She had to stop him in his tracks. With her adrenaline pumping, her heart pounding wildly, she forgot her pain just a bit. She knew she had to get out of the cemetery and to her car.

Peering over the headstone, she saw the man limping and leaning on another headstone, crouching slightly. She guessed he was tending to his existing wound, pressing on it, staunching the blood flow. She couldn't afford to show mercy. As thoughts ran through her mind of little baby William, and Claire, she pointed her gun and fired again. Just as the man crumpled in a heap, she heard Troy call out, "Maddie! Stay down!"

She leaned against a cold headstone. She could see Troy emerge from the shadows, his face bruised, gun drawn.

At least they were both safe. Alive.

It was only now, with the rush of adrenaline slowed, that she began shaking in earnest. It wasn't the cold. It was the reality that inside of two weeks, her life had been turned upside down. With startling clarity, she realized that she, Madison Taylor-Pruitt, heiress to one of America's biggest fortunes, may just have killed her first man.

Chapter 13

Madison called in sick the next day—and her father was none too pleased.

"Goddamnit, Madison, what the hell is going on with you? Bing is breathing down my neck over the board meeting, the board itself is up in arms, the police have been here yet again with a search warrant for Claire's office, and meanwhile, you're goddamn AWOL. How do you think that looks?"

"How does it look? It looks like I'm sick and can't come in."

"Don't give me that."

Madison couldn't believe how her normally cool-headed father was losing it.

"Dad, I've been working for you for years now, and I came to work with double pneumonia last winter. So it's not like I take it lightly. I just am really not feeling well. I think it's stomach flu. Maybe food poisoning."

"You want me to send over Dr. Halloway?"

"No."

"Might as well make him earn his salary."

"No," she said more insistently.

"Look…are you pulling this because of Claire? Because your job, Madison, has nothing to do with my personal life. You have—"

"A responsibility to our shareholders." She said it singsong fashion.

"That's not funny. You think your position as future CEO here is a joke?"

"No. It's just that someone I loved, someone you claimed to love, was murdered. And you're more interested in Wall Street than seeing her killer brought to justice."

"You act like you're thirteen years old, Madison. Like you're some petulant teen, instead of responsible for hundreds of millions of dollars and major shareholder decisions and obligations. I've always had to put aside my feelings. And so have you. Now, suddenly, you're acting completely out of character. I'll expect you here tomorrow, acting like you support me to the fullest, Madison. I'm counting on you, but if you don't care about that—and it appears you don't—then the company is counting on you. If we take a major market dive, then people, employees, who have given their years in dedication and service to us, will be out of jobs. That can be on your conscience."

"And I wonder what's on your conscience, Dad."

"What the hell is that supposed to mean?"

"Figure it out," she snapped and hung up the phone. She soon felt guilty. She could sense her father's growing desperation as his world—ordinarily so controlled—spun out of his control.

Her cell phone rang. She saw it was John Hernandez, calling from his cell.

"Madison?"

"Hi, John."

"I've been worried about you. You didn't come to the homework session yesterday. Actually, that's not entirely true. I was worried, but then I started to wonder if you were just avoiding me."

Madison cursed herself in her mind. She had meant to call him, but the two thugs at the cemetery had effectively taken care of that.

"How could you think that? What am I saying? I know it was bad form of me not to show or call…and I am so, so sorry. I had a wonderful time. A better than wonderful time. I ran into some work issues, and then I got food poisoning. I've been in bed."

"Do you want me to come over and take care of you? I could whip up a pot of chicken soup."

"No…I'm really miserable company right now." She purposely made her voice sound a little weak.

"My bed seems empty without you."

Madison felt a bolt of warmth sear through her. "You have no idea how much I wish I was there."

"When can I see you?"

"How about Saturday night?"

"Sounds great. I'll call you to check on you in a day or so. Feel better. And I'll see you Saturday."

"Okay…bye."

"Bye, angel."

Madison hung up the phone. For a brief moment, she let herself recall the moment when he slid inside her. It was like her body was made to fit his. Shaking the thought from her mind, she checked her watch. Troy was due over in about fifteen minutes to reconvene a strategy as far as investigating Claire's murder—and the box of clues.

She padded into her kitchen and started a pot of

coffee. She wore a yoga outfit from Christy Turling-ton's Nuala line. Madison's mother was a huge yoga fanatic—for a while. Like most everything, Chantal had eventually grown bored and gave it up. Madison still tried to at least begin each day with some stretches, but this morning, every bit of her hurt. The yoga clothes were a simple nod to comfort.

Fifteen minutes later, her doorman called her and said a Mr. Carter was there. She told him to send him up, and she opened the door when Troy arrived.

"Whew," he said, letting out a low whistle. "So this is how the heir to the Pruitt fortune lives." He walked to the bank of windows and gazed out on Central Park. The crisp fall day showed off the colors of the trees.

"Give me a break. Renee is hardly living the poor life and you're there all the time. Around many beautiful agents. A lot of men would kill for your job."

"A lot of men kill for the fun of it."

"You know what I mean. Tell me you haven't gotten used to Renee's chef's watercress salad and warm pomegranate vinaigrette. There must be FBI agents in the field just green with envy."

He nodded, smiling. "Working with Renee and you is a cushy deal, I admit it. Still, that's like my make-believe life. Agents don't live like this in the off-hours, Madison."

No, she thought looking around her apartment. In one corner stood an armoire from eighteenth-century France in a burled wood and polished to a sheen. She had bid sixty thousand dollars for it at Sotheby's. *And I suppose teachers don't live like this either.*

Thinking of John made her frown. She turned her head and said, "I'm going to go get us some coffee."

"Great…I could use it. I'll help."

He followed her into her expansive kitchen as she busied herself pulling out china and sugar. She favored raw cane sugar and a tea biscuit or two.

"What's the matter?" Troy asked her. "Your face clouded up in there a minute or so ago."

"It's nothing."

"Come on. It has to be something."

"Perceptive of you."

"Training. I took a profiling course—a bunch of them actually—at Quantico. I was pretty good at it. Then I got too old."

"What do you mean, too old?"

"The best profilers are under twenty-eight."

"Why?"

"The older you get, the more you make allowances."

Madison put the mugs and silver coffeepot and sugar bowl on a teak tray and pulled a carton of cream from the subzero refrigerator. Troy lifted the tray and carried it to the dining room.

"What do you mean, allowances?"

"Well, when you're eighteen, say, and you meet someone, what's your typical reaction?… I'll tell you. A teen makes a snap decision. Dork or cool guy. Nerd or jock. Outcast or cheerleader. They see the world in instantaneous black and white. When we get older, we temper that. We learn there's more to someone than appearance and body language."

"Isn't that a good thing?" Madison sat down and poured them both coffee. Troy sat opposite her.

"It is. I mean, certainly in a philosophical sense it is. But here's the thing, that's still part of how a young person's brain works. It's more impulsive. I've even seen studies about almost a shearing effect as the brain goes through growth spurts. New, fast, impulsive pathways are born. It's all very new science. Anyway…the bottom line is the younger a profiler is, usually the more talented. I wasn't meant to stay a profiler. I ended up with this special assignment."

"But you still have the skills. You picked up that something was wrong."

"Yeah." He held her gaze. "Come on…spill."

"I was just wondering, I guess, how to balance

being an agent with being a…person. I mean, for one thing, I am responsible for so much in my job. I've been chained to my desk for so long—because I love it, but also because I always felt I had something I wanted to prove. That my name wasn't the reason for my success. That my talent was."

"It's a balancing act, that's for sure."

"But then, I also have this new relationship." Madison saw a cloud of disappointment skate across Troy's face.

"Uh-huh."

"Well…I'm doing an awful lot of lying. To hide my double life. I feel like it's going to be impossible to be one person with him and another with the Gotham Roses."

"I won't lie to you. A lot of marriages and relationships just don't work once people start with the agency. It's just too complicated."

"I thought so," Madison said, sipping her coffee.

"That's not to say it *couldn't* work. It's just to say that there's a lot of pressure, and it is hard to explain certain things away. I have two friends in the CIA, and they pretty much have given up on relationships. I mean, how can you be with someone if they can never ask you about your job, where you're going, what you're doing for a living, that whole thing."

"I'm just feeling a little overwhelmed. All this undercover stuff makes a day in the boardroom seem like a picnic. Like last night in Venetian Lake—I mean the adrenaline rush was so intense compared to the boardroom. I've known men to throw up before board meetings because it's so pressurized. But I thrive on it. I love a challenge, which I guess is why I feel cut out for this Gotham Rose thing no matter how intense it gets. Speaking of which, what's the status on those two guys?"

"They'll both make it, though the one you got in the chest, the bullet pierced his lung and lodged in his back. He'll be out of commission for a long time yet."

Madison tried to process the information that she had wounded someone seriously. "Have you questioned them yet?" she asked softly.

"No. They're both in a morphine haze. One is in intensive care—the one with the pierced lung. It'll be a while before we get anything substantive out of him." Troy took a swig of coffee. "Do you have the box from Claire."

Madison nodded. Troy seemed unfazed by the events at Venetian Lake—even though he was sporting a major welt on his face. She pulled the box out from under the table and laid the contents out for them both to look at.

"First of all," Madison said, "I think she did it this way to protect me. If she didn't spell it out completely, then if someone broke in my apartment there'd be nothing for him to find. Her mother would be safe, too. So it's like a puzzle. A travel brochure from the Caymans. Well, you said it was likely some of this had to do with shell companies if the mob was involved—laundering money. And the seashell—represents the Caymans *and* the shell companies."

"Okay, I'm with you there."

"A key. To what? Well, it's not an apartment key—and to be honest, I have a key to her place— and she had one to mine. We were best friends. So she would know that I would instantly realize this wasn't to anything obvious there. So, coupled with the other clues, I'm guessing a safe-deposit box at a bank in the Caymans."

"Makes sense," Troy said.

"A photo of the Manhattan skyline, well, that's kind of obvious. She was murdered at the site of our new tower-construction project, so it must have something to do with that. And when she was killed, she wouldn't have known that she would be found dead there, so this was her clue. Just in case."

"And her passport." Troy took the green passport

book and opened it. "She went to the Caymans twice in the last three months of her life. Did you know that?'

Madison shook her head. "No."

"Was that usual? I mean, that she wouldn't tell you."

"Well, it wouldn't have been usual—before our falling-out. But even so, my father didn't go with her, and they were fairly inseparable. That is odd."

"And finally, a map with Venetian Lake marked. Like you said last night, what could it all possibly have to do with the old murder of your uncle? An infant kidnapped more than fifty years ago. His kidnapper long dead in prison."

"I'm no closer to an answer. And the safe-deposit key, there's no account number, no way to know what it's to for sure."

"Let's think."

Maddie and Troy, almost as if the items were talismans, each picked them up one at a time. Maddie willed Claire to speak to her, to make it all clear, but she was as confused as ever.

And then, like the sun suddenly breaking through a storm cloud, Maddie grew excited.

"Oh, my God! I get it! At least part of it."

"Want to clue me in?"

Maddie nodded. "Why would Claire include the seashell?"

"Like you said. Representing shell companies. And the Caymans."

"Maybe, but—" Madison turned the conch shell over in her hands and pulled it very close to her face. "I was right…" She grinned. "Looks like I am cut out for this work."

"Okay, 007, let me know what you figured out."

"Claire knows I used to love doing the *New York Times* Sunday crossword puzzle, and my favorite ones had puns or tricks to them. Well, this shell is nothing more than a trick. A five-letter word for whisperer of ocean secrets."

"I don't get it."

Madison smiled, feeling her excitement grow.

"Claire knew she didn't have to be obvious with me. Eventually, I would figure it out. I don't need a clue as obvious as a seashell. I don't need a clue for the Caymans, since the travel brochure is there. So what else can a big conch shell like this do?"

"Provide shelter for a conch."

"Right. Shelter. Tax shelter. Okay. And if you hold a conch to your ear, what will it do?"

"It won't do anything."

"It will duplicate the ocean's roar, though. You

can hear the sea. It's as if it can tell you something. A secret." Maddie handed Troy the shell. "Look inside."

"Holy shit!" Troy exclaimed.

For there, etched into the soft pink hue of the conch's interior shell, was engraved the name of a bank in the Caymans, along with a safe-deposit-box number.

Chapter 14

"Oh, my God! Look at me," Maddie exclaimed as she stared in the three-way mirror and twirled slowly around. Claire's reflection stared back at her.

"Pretty amazing what we can do, huh?" Troy asked her.

"It's uncanny."

The papers that week had been filled with innuendo and gossip about her father refusing to take a lie detector test—through his attorneys, of course, a high-powered team that threatened to devour the police detectives and the media. The lawyers spoke in sound bites and the war of words was just beginning, Madison knew. The media were like sharks in waters filled with fresh chum.

The Pruitt & Pruitt board had agreed to convene the next week to determine a course of action until the investigation was completed. Her uncle Bing— a major shareholder—and her father were edgy and sending assistants scurrying and cowering into their offices. In the meantime, Maddie and Troy were flying to the Caymans on Thursday night, and had an appointment at the bank on Friday morning.

Maddie needed a cover story for her absence from the office. The case and all its intricacies was taking up a lot of her time—at a point when she really couldn't afford to be out of the office. Maddie decided to say she was going to Miami to view a property she'd been eyeing before Claire's murder. She would bring Troy to see if the site was viable for a hotel.

Now at the town house, Madison was literally transformed into Claire.

Kristi Burke was the stylist for the Gotham Roses. Her job was to give the women working undercover whatever look they needed to complete their assignments. She walked around Madison, obsessing over every detail.

"I have given girls complete makeovers. They've

been transformed into everything from call girls to foreign dignitaries. Blondes to brunettes and back again. Redheads in every shade of the color spectrum. I've taught them to walk the catwalk for one assignment, and how to wrap a sari for another. But this…this is the pièce de résistance. It's unbelievable."

Madison smoothed the sleek line of her black bob—an expensive wig. Her hands trembled slightly. It felt almost sacrilegious to portray Claire, and a vague queasy feeling passed over Madison. On the other hand, by portraying her, she could access the safe-deposit box and perhaps solve this case once and for all, hopefully while saving the corporation in the same action.

Kristi, dressed in a funky Anna Sui tweed jacket and miniskirt in a soft green that showed off her auburn hair, shook her head. "I'm amazed. What do you think, Troy?"

"Kristi, you're a genius. I even asked Renee to come down."

Almost as if on cue, Renee swept into the dressing room. She stopped and shook her head in amazement.

"It's uncanny."

"Thanks," Kristi said. "Colored contacts, perfect

makeup job—I altered her lip line completely into the cupid's bow, like the photo Madison brought of her. Cindy Crawford–mole drawn here," she pointed. "A wig to die for. The right clothes. Changed her eyebrows a bit—more arched. Gives her the cat's-eye kind of appearance. Exotic."

Renee approached Madison. "How do you feel?" She clasped her hand, empathy registering on her face. "I'm sure this isn't easy, darling."

"Thanks for asking. It isn't. It actually feels very, very strange…and sad."

"You're doing a superb job. I briefed the Governess's representative on this one. The concern is an Enron-type blowup over at Pruitt & Pruitt. But the powers that be are impressed by your prowess so far. We chose well."

Madison wasn't sure she believed in this phantom "Governess." In fact, she definitely didn't. But figuring out who was the mystery person pulling strings behind the Gotham Roses was a far lower priority, behind catching Claire's killer.

"She was born for this," Troy said. He looked at his watch. "Time to grab our limo, Claire."

Madison froze imperceptibly at the name, but then, without missing a beat, said, "Great. Let's go."

Leaving through a side entrance where a sleek,

black, dark-tinted limo waited, Madison and Troy climbed in the back while Renee's chauffeur put their overnight bags in the trunk. Madison's was a Louis Vuitton and Troy's a black duffel bag—what a mismatched pair, Madison thought. The chauffeur climbed behind the wheel, pulled into traffic and headed toward the United Nations area and then onward to Long Island and LaGuardia Airport.

With the privacy glass up between them and the driver, Madison said, "Can I ask you something...? Who is the Governess, anyway?"

"No one knows."

"Renee told me that, but I figured she was just keeping me in the dark. You know, until I proved myself."

"Hell, you've already proved yourself. I can tell you're determined to see this through to the end, no matter who turns out to be behind it. No...Renee doesn't know who the Governess is. And neither do I."

"You have any hunches?"

"No. I mean, sometimes I think it might be Attorney General Cleghorn. Other times I guess someone from the president's cabinet, other times the second-in-command at the bureau. Bottom line? I haven't a clue."

"Don't you find all this cloak-and-dagger stuff a little weird?"

"I used to. But then I realized there was a whole shadow realm to the government, to law enforcement, to the world, that most don't know about—and to catch the really bad guys, you need all the weapons you can muster in your arsenal. Hence the Gotham Roses. Just a prettier, classier weapon, but a weapon nonetheless. You know, people used to think that white-collar crime wasn't so bad, wasn't worth going after. The Savings and Loan scandals, the junk-bond kings, insider trading. But now that so many ordinary citizens have money in mutual funds, company stocks, IRAs, retirement accounts…so they can send their kids to college, people realize a few bad apples can literally wipe out whole families' meager savings, decimate the confidence of investors. The administration knows this is bad for politics. It's bad for the country."

"Well, I also didn't give my heart and soul to my company to watch some unseen bastard destroy it. Let's go catch some bad guys," Madison said as they crossed into Long Island. She didn't care who the Governess was. Hell, it could be her grandmother for all she cared. She just wanted whoever was responsible for Claire's death—and the big lump on the back of her head—to pay.

* * *

"Ms. Shipley," the bank manager said, sweeping his head down to kiss her hand, "a pleasure to see you again."

"Thank you. Lovely to see you, as well."

"And what can we do for you today?"

"I'd like to visit my safe-deposit box."

"But of course. Follow me."

Madison and Troy had arrived the night before on the small island, a territory of the United Kingdom. Madison walked behind the bank manager. He had on a crisp blue blazer and a tie reminiscent of the sort worn at Eton. Gray slacks, expensive loafers. Very preppie. He had an uppercrust British accent, no doubt sent to boarding school, Madison imagined.

He led her into the vault area, and she produced her key.

"Excellent," he said. He pulled out some papers. "A formality, but sign here, as always."

Madison had practiced Claire's signature over and over again all the previous night. She took a breath to calm herself. Troy had told her on the plane flight over that the manager would accept her at face value. Three visits hardly meant he knew Claire intimately. *Relax,* she told herself as she lifted the Mark Cross pen. *He hasn't an idea you're not Claire.*

Indeed, the manager didn't even *look* at her signature. He pulled out a large safe-deposit box, gave her a gracious half bow and said, "Simply press the button when you're through."

"Merci," Madison said. Claire had always used that…and her standard goodbye was *Au revoir.* She wasn't French—just a silly habit, Claire used to tell her. Her French tutor had ingrained it into her as a child.

Once the manager left the vault, Madison opened the box. Inside were papers, neatly bundled with rubber bands, sheaves of them nestled against each other. She pulled one out and took off the rubber band. They were copies of ledger pages and computer printouts of accounts. Shell companies. There was no way Madison could make sense of it immediately, but she assumed this was the evidence she needed—the evidence Claire died for. Troy told her that the agency had forensics accountants ready to pore over anything on the waterfront-tower property at a moment's notice.

Madison put every single paper into the alligator-skin briefcase she'd brought with her, pressed the button to exit the vault, and proceeded to the bank lobby, her heels clicking on the pink marble. Troy was waiting, and they took a cab back to their hotel.

They were staying on the beach, in rooms opposite each other. Both had ocean views from their
balcony, and the Caymans at this time of year were
magnificent—the waters bluer than ever, the temperature perfect, without humidity.

Once inside the hotel, they went to Madison's
room and spread all the papers out on the bed.

"Does any of this make sense to you?" Troy
asked.

"Not really. Not yet. But give me a couple of
hours."

"We have five hours until we have to leave for the
airport. In the meantime, I'm going to place a few
calls to get the accountants ready for us at Renee's."

Troy let himself out, and Madison called room
service and asked for a club sandwich and a Diet
Coke to be sent up. Then she settled in to pore over
the papers.

It was like entering a maze. She couldn't believe
that her own company could have so many accounts
for, at least on the surface of things, bogus subsidi-
aries. She felt sick to her stomach. The S.E.C. im-
plications alone would be enough to send shock
waves through the stock exchange.

She massaged her temples. What a mess!

And then she took the rubber bands off a sheaf of

papers that looked like canceled payroll checks. Madison felt even sicker. Because there was the signature of a William Charles Pruitt III. The little baby buried in the family vault. He had a social security number, and apparently, he'd been drawing several different salaries over the years at Pruitt & Pruitt.

A dead person on the payroll.

With the title of senior vice president.

Maddie leaped from the bed and went to run across the hall to tell Troy. His hotel-room door was ever so slightly ajar. From inside she could hear sounds of a struggle.

Panic swept over her. Troy had declared to security that he was an agent before the flight, and he had been allowed to check his sidearm, unloaded, through customs and security. But the Gotham Roses undercover agency was, ostensibly, a shadow one. Renee had explained to her on her orientation day that in some situations, this secretive nature would operate against them. For instance, she couldn't identify herself as an agent on the flight. So she had no weapon. This hadn't seemed like a problem with Troy along at the bank, but it sure as hell was a problem now.

Well, Madison thought, *time to see if what Jimmy Valentine taught me works in a real situation.*

She inhaled deeply, gathered her energy into her solar plexus, the way she'd been taught, and kicked the door open, surprising the man who was choking Troy. With a flying sidekick, she kicked the man as hard as she could in the side, knocking him over. Troy fell to the floor, looking, at least to Madison, as if he was dead.

"I thought you were killed," the man growled as he stared up at her. "I saw you. You were dead." His eyes were wide, and Madison thought he looked spooked.

Taking advantage of his shock, she kicked a foot to his face. He grabbed it though, pushing her backward. Falling against the small hotel table, Madison lost her balance. She and the bastard who'd killed Claire both scrambled to their feet. She used Jimmy Valentine's leg-sweep method to bring him down again. Then she added a sharp kick to his diaphragm, knocking the wind out of him.

Wasting no time, she kicked his windpipe, and leaned hard with her foot on his throat. She heard a sort of sickening whistle. Then he clawed at her leg. He was gurgling, fighting for air, and she leaned down her weight more. Finally, the man passed out. She ran to the bedside table, lifted the lamp, and came back and smashed it on his head for good measure. Then she raced to Troy and felt for a pulse. It was there, a little weak, but there.

She didn't know if she should call for an ambulance. She was essentially in a foreign nation with an FBI agent and a man she'd just single-handedly beaten up. She stood and went to the bathroom, wetting a towel with cold water and coming back to Troy and pressing it on his head. In a minute or two—during which she tried to fight her fears—he started to rouse. He coughed, and then his eyelids fluttered.

"What happened?" he croaked.

"I'm not sure. I saw your door open a bit, came in, and that guy—" she pointed to the man on the floor "—was choking you until you passed out."

"Jesus…" He sat up and rubbed his throat, which was very red. "Can you get me a glass of water? And shut the door in case someone walks by."

Madison did as he asked. Then Troy stood and looked down on the man. "Do you recognize him?"

The guy on the floor was extremely well-built, almost to the point of being muscle-bound, with close-cropped dark hair and a square jaw. He had a scar near his left eye, and a single diamond stud earring.

"No. But he recognized me…um, Claire. He said that he had seen me—dead."

Troy leaned down and felt the man's carotid. "He's still alive."

Troy rolled the man on his side and found his wallet. "No ID."

"What's that?"

"What?"

Maddie knelt down and rolled up the man's sleeve. "Look. A tattoo."

"I've never seen anything like that." It was an intricate dagger—truly a work of art.

"It's Russian."

"What does it say along the dagger?"

"Kremlin Killers."

"Mob. They're infiltrating some of New York's drug trade, not to mention Moscow and some of the fallen Eastern European countries. Heavy into the prostitution biz. Drugs. Murder for hire."

"So what do we do with this guy?"

"We call the local authorities. I also have to call in to my boss at the Bureau. Oh, and hey, thanks for saving my life. He caught me off guard."

"Well, I owed you. Now we're even."

"Not by a long shot, but thank God you came across the hall."

"I had something to tell you."

Maddie explained to him about the accounts for William Pruitt.

"Shit, Madison...we're going to have our hands full with the forensic accountants."

"No kidding. Listen, you call the police. I'm going to pack...eat something. Get ready. Now that I did what I need to, can I change out of my Claire look?"

"No. You need it for your seat on the return flight. Since 9/11, it's a lot trickier for us to fly commercial and make changes. Use her passport, same as on the way here."

"All right, but as soon as we land, I'm losing the wig. It's itching me like mad." Because it had been put on expertly by the stylist, Madison was afraid to take it off and put it back on herself.

"You got it."

Maddie left Troy's room and headed over to her own. Once inside, she opened the minibar and took out a little vodka bottle. She poured it into a glass and swallowed it in one swig to settle her nerves.

Kremlin Killers.

What the hell had Pruitt & Pruitt gotten mixed up in?

Chapter 15

In The Know With Rubi Cho

So is one of our city's fairest heiresses finally
getting some much-needed R&R?

The lovely and always perfectly put-to-
gether American heiress, Madison Taylor-
Pruitt was snapped at JFK airport in this photo
with a hunky assistant. Business or pleasure?

Our poor Madison has been chained to her
desk for far too long, and with the police closing in on Jack Pruitt, and Madison being eyed

for even greater responsibility, we can only applaud her. Head to the islands—or the slopes of Aspen—our dear Madison. We think it's high time you remembered you're one of the city's most eligible bachelorettes.

Chapter 16

Madison awoke on Saturday, checked her e-mail from the office by hookup from her apartment, attended to her electronic scheduler, left voice mails for about three dozen employees and enjoyed two cups of coffee. Then she saw her picture in Rubi's column. After the flight, she had gone into the ladies room in the airport and taken off her wig. Her hair was matted and flat, but it felt good to run a brush through it. Then she pulled it back into a ponytail and headed to baggage claim with Troy. By chance, a photographer spotted her and snapped away.

At 11:00 a.m. the phone rang—an interior phone from the concierge or front desk.

"Hello?"

"Ms. Pruitt, there's a John Hernandez here."

"What?"

"Yes, ma'am. And he's parked his motorcycle outside. Is that all right, ma'am?"

"Um…yes. Oh, dear…" Madison was completely flustered. He had to have seen the paper. Rubi's column wasn't in the financial section—it was way up front.

"Shall I send him up?"

"Yes, do. Oh…God, what a mess."

Madison ran to the bathroom. Her hair was pulled up in a loose ponytail, she had on no makeup, and she was dressed in her yoga outfit.

"Damn!" she said to her reflection. The last two weeks or so were starting to take their toll. She swiped some concealer under her eyes to get rid of the dark circles, but there wasn't time to do anything else.

The doorbell to her apartment rang, and Madison's hands started shaking.

"Great," she muttered, "I can practically kill a man with my bare hands, but at the thought of seeing this guy, I'm mush."

She went to the apartment door and opened it. John stood there, looking gorgeous in a black sweater and worn jeans that showed off his well-muscled legs. He was holding a copy of the newspaper open to Rubi Cho's column. And fury was registered on his face.

"That's not a very good picture of me," Madison offered, trying to defuse the situation, smiling halfheartedly.

"So let me get this straight. I'm good enough to *fuck,* but apparently, I'm not good enough to tell even the first thing about your life to."

She recoiled at the curse, as if she'd been physically slapped. She'd never heard him use curse words before. "That's not how it is, John."

"Isn't it? This guy—" he thrust the paper toward her "—he looks like he'd fit in with your life on Central Park West."

"It was business. Please…please come in. If I had it to do over again, I swear to you I'd have told you right from the beginning."

John shook his head. "I've been played," he said and started to turn.

Madison grabbed his arm. "Please…you haven't been played. I was just too scared to tell you the truth."

Jaw clenched, he half faced her. "Scared? To admit you were rich?"

"Please just let me explain. Please?"

"And what about this guy?" He held up the paper.

"Please? Come in, and I'll explain."

John shook her off his arm, but he did follow her into the apartment. This was worse than the most vicious board meeting, Madison decided. She was used to fighting people through her lawyers, through her public-relations team. She was used to veiled digs and slights on the social ladder. She was even used to blind items in Rubi Cho's column. But this was a man who wore his fury right out there. Given what they'd shared in bed, Madison told herself she should have assumed he'd fight just as passionately.

She watched as his eyes registered her apartment. "Renovations?" he sneered, apparently recalling why she said her place was off-limits. "You just didn't want me parking a Harley outside your lobby."

"That's not it. Sit down," she urged.

He sat on the couch, but leaned forward, as if he was most definitely not going to get comfortable. He tossed the paper on the coffee table, right next to a Fabergé egg. Then he clasped his hands together tightly.

Maddie remained standing, and she started pacing, trying to gather her thoughts.

"When I started working at the charter school, I wanted to just be me. Not some heiress…I wanted to be in the classroom, interacting with kids, not being treated with kid gloves myself. Mr. Hayes, the principal, he agreed to honor that and was very supportive. I was also able to fund computers and do all sorts of amazing things through the Pruitt Family Trust, and I got to do it basically anonymously. At school, I was Ms. *Taylor,* not Pruitt. I wasn't there to elevate myself, John. I was there to make a difference. Quietly."

He wasn't looking at her. He was staring at some unseen spot on the oriental rug, his eyes intense.

She rushed on, headlong, into her story. "Then I met you. It was the highlight of my week—every week. But I felt like I had the Maddie who worked with the kids and you, and the Maddie who was running Pruitt & Pruitt's real-estate division. And they were two parts that would never meet, so why bother telling you all about my 'poor little rich girl' life."

She took a breath, then continued. "The more you told me about your upbringing, the less I felt like I could tell you about mine. It was hopelessly lonely, and I was raised by nannies and shuttled off to boarding schools with other lonely kids. But it wasn't about gangs and life and death on the streets. In my own way, I admired you…and was embarrassed by some of the excesses of my life. I mean, I won't pretend that I don't love going to Sotheby's and bidding on a painting or spending the weekend in Paris, but I just couldn't face your scorn."

"Scorn?" He looked up with hurt and anger registering in his eyes. "Why would I treat you with scorn, Madison? Why would I judge you like that? I don't like to be judged for my Harley or my tattoos, so why would I judge someone else?"

Madison looked at him pleadingly. "I don't know. I just couldn't imagine you accepting that I live in this life and run a huge conglomerate, and you live your quieter life of meaning. I figured you would either be intimidated or would hate me for being rich."

"Or maybe you thought I'd just be after your money."

"I never once thought that!" Her own anger flared.

"Don't give me that," he snapped. "I'm sure it ran through your mind."

"Never once! Damn you! Never once."

"Well, then what about being embarrassed by me? Maybe you just don't think I'm good enough to be seen out with you. I mean, you kept me away from your apartment, your life, the restaurants and places where you're seen…you would come to Harlem to avoid being seen with me."

"That's just not true. I would never be embarrassed by you. Ever. But you were so…gallant. I mean, you wanted to pay for my cabs…how could I take you somewhere I usually go and ask you to pay for a sixty-dollar Blue Pearl martini? I could just imagine what would run through your mind. That I was spoiled. And that sixty dollars could buy a whole lot of school supplies."

She watched his face and saw a slight softening. She regarded that as an opening, much as she watched opponents at the negotiating table for signs their position might be weakening.

"I don't know what to think, Maddie. I mean, you lied to me."

She went to him and knelt down between his legs. She loosened his hands from each other with her own, then slipped her hands into his palms. "I just wanted what I had with you to be real. If you only knew what I faced every day—the backstabbing, the vicious negotiations. The social climbing. And I could have faced telling you about my world, but I guess I wanted to wait until we felt solid, without having to raise the ugly issues."

"What ugly issues?"

"Let's say we go on from here…I still go to your place. Will you come here?"

He hesitated. "I guess."

"Fine. And when I have to go to a black-tie function, will you come with me? Will it bother you that we travel by limo and I'm whipping out a black American Express card, and that I have to fly away on business on a moment's notice?"

"Look, Madison, I hadn't thought that far."

"Exactly. But would it bother your pride if I could give us some amazing things—different things from your life. I mean, John, no one ever cooked for me my whole life—other than our family chef. You gave me that gift. I loved that date. And I can give us other things, but I know in terms of what you might think, in terms of ego, or…you know at these functions, you'll meet people who will act appalled that you're a teacher. That you're not 'one of us.' I didn't want to subject you to that right away. I wanted us to have a real shot, John. I don't know if I thought that at first. I only knew that when I would go to your school on Mondays, I felt like some schoolgirl with a crush. And when you're someone who routinely closes deals worth hundreds of millions of dollars, that's not a very comfortable feeling."

He finally looked her in the eye. "No more lying?"

She took her finger and crossed her left breast. "Cross my heart."

Without warning, he grabbed her and pulled her to his chest, almost lifting her to him, and kissed her. "I was sick riding over here, Madison. I can't get you out from under my skin. I'm crazy for you."

Yet again, she was amazed at the ferocity of their connection. She kissed him back, straddling his lap and putting a hand on each side of his face. Hurriedly, he pulled off her top, kissing first one breast then the other.

"Let's go to bed," Madison said huskily. She slid off his lap and led him by the hand to her bedroom. They each undressed and climbed under the chilly sheets. She hadn't opened the blinds that morning, so they were cocooned in the semidark coolness of the room.

She pushed up against him and then lifted her thigh over the top of him, sliding up so she was on top. She pulled the ponytail band out of her hair and let it cascade down, leaning over and tickling his chest with the ends of her hair.

He pushed her back a bit, staring up at her face. "You're my angel, you know."

She nodded and looked down at him. He was so extraordinarily masculine, so powerful. "You're mine."

She slid farther back, then took him and slid him inside her. Both of them moaned at once. He grabbed her wrists and pulled her down so he could breathe in her ear, letting her hear how much she drove him wild. At the sounds of his building orgasm, she grew more turned on until she swore it was as if they had shut out the rest of the entire world and were lost in this sexual space that was unlike any she'd experienced before.

When they were done, they were both sweaty and completely spent. She climbed off him and then nestled against him. "Please don't leave today."

"Never."

And soon, Madison was sleeping soundly next to John, feeling safer than she had in weeks. Maybe her whole life.

Chapter 17

Madison and John had dinner at Nobu. They took his Harley—but her American Express card. And they had a great time.

"I've never had sushi before," he said shyly.

"Let me order for us, then, okay?"

He nodded, and she placed their order, choosing milder fish she thought a beginner might like. They drank hot sake, and then a cold filtered one. Madison felt downright giddy. All the time she had been dreading John discovering her wealth, she'd never stopped to think about all the fun they could have

spending it. She imagined trips and dinners and ski-
ing and weekends at the beach over the summer.

"You look happy," he said. "I like it when you
smile."

"It's just such a relief not to have this secret between us. I feel like a hundred-pound weight has
been lifted from my chest. And I love the idea that
we can have Manhattan as a playground together."

"As long as I get to play with you, then I don't
mind, angel."

"You know, when you say things like that…I
get…so turned on."

"Dessert at your place?"

She nodded. When dinner was over, they rode
back to her building and made love again.

"Stay the night?" she asked him, leaning up on
one elbow and tracing her fingers along his chest.
She thought back in her mind—she had never asked
a man to spend the night before. She was always
working in her home office late into the night—staying the night would be inconvenient. But with John,
she just didn't care.

"Can't, angel. I've got to get up really early to
face a classroom full of teens tomorrow. What about
tomorrow night you stay over after tutoring?"

"Can't. Have you read in the papers about the murder of Pruitt & Pruitt's legal counsel?"

"Vaguely. It didn't register before, you know? I don't pay much attention to anything having to do with Wall Street. I don't watch the news—I'm usually going over lesson plans."

"She was my best friend. And she was murdered. And my father is a suspect."

"What?" He narrowed his eyes and looked at her in the flickering light of a candle they'd lit.

"It's a really ugly story, but the bottom line is, they were lovers and they hid the affair from me. When she died, she and I were estranged. I don't think my father killed her. I don't think he hired someone to do it. But the fact remains that until the police do find out who did it, our company's stock will go down unless he is replaced as CEO and chairman. He wants me to be the new CEO…and my uncle Bing wants to be CEO."

"What do you want?"

"Well, I find Bing out of touch with the employees. He's just not the person to lead us forward, I don't think. And I've been groomed for this my whole life."

"Then you should go for it.… I understand about tomorrow. What about later in the week?"

"You don't happen to own a tux, do you?"

"No, Madison. I don't have a tux hanging in my closet. Don't have much call for one in my line of work." He reached around and pinched her backside.

"Ouch," she said, laughing. "Well, what if I was to send you to my father's tailor and have him fit you for one pronto? Could you escort me to a little party on Thursday and then maybe stay over?"

"Sure. What kind of little party?"

"Oh…a fund-raiser."

"What kind of fund-raiser?" he asked, playfully suspicious.

"Oh, you know…for New York senator Ellie Richardson."

"Please tell me you're kidding."

She shook her head. "No, I'm not."

"Sure, I'll go. But if I get Senator Richardson alone for two minutes, I'm going to ask her why she's cut funding for education."

Madison laughed. "Good for you! You do that. But she's no pushover."

"That's all right. Neither am I."

Bing was furious. Madison could see it in his eyes. The board had voted to "temporarily" ask Jack Pruitt to step down until the "cloud of suspicion surrounding the death of Claire Shipley is resolved, though the board has every confidence in his innocence." The press release went on to state, "In the interim, the board has named Madison Taylor-Pruitt as acting CEO. Ms. Taylor-Pruitt has proved herself a capable and visionary leader, and we have no doubt this decision is the one to steer our corporation and shareholders in the twenty-first century."

Bing asked her to step into his office after the board meeting.

"Shut the door."

Madison did as he asked, bracing herself for the confrontation. Her uncle was a near-twin of her father, though his hairline receded a bit and his hair was all silver. He stood about six feet tall, and had the build of a former world-class diver—broad shoulders and lean physique.

"I hope you're satisfied with your little coup d'état," he hissed. He was always condescending to everyone.

"It wasn't a coup, Bing. This company needs energetic leadership, and for right now, we need a smooth transition."

"Look…you can fool them all, but you and your father can't fool me. I think this entire disgrace has been orchestrated."

"I won't even dignify that with a response. Claire is dead. That's hardly an orchestrated act simply to win a seat as CEO, Bing. When you calm down, then we'll talk."

Madison turned on her heel.

"I'm not through with you, young lady. Don't you dare walk out on me."

"Well, I'm done with you. And as new CEO, I have a busy agenda."

She walked out of his office and slammed the door behind her.

"What's wrong, Madison?" Bing's administrative assistant asked her.

"Nothing, Katherine. He's just clearly unhappy with the board's decision."

Katherine Gould nodded. She was about fifty, and Madison always thought she was truly elegant. She worked her hair into a ballerina topknot each day, accentuating her high cheekbones, and Madison knew Bing gave her a clothing allowance. He was absolutely convinced that only the most impeccable assistant should greet anyone he did business with—it reflected on him, just as, Madison was sure, he felt the present scandal reflected on him as well.

"He's been under a great deal of stress lately," she whispered.

"We all have, Katherine."

"I know…but…" Katherine looked completely torn.

"What?"

"I don't know if I should tell you, though as new CEO…"

"Katherine, whatever you say to me, I will hold in strictest confidence. I've always had an open-door policy with my people. And by that I mean this entire company, from the cleaning crew to my executives."

Katherine's eyes welled. "What if it had to do with your father?"

Madison tried not to reveal her emotions. "If he's in trouble, Katherine, it's my duty as CEO—and as his daughter—to help him, while at the same time not letting it affect the company as a whole."

Katherine nodded and bit her lip. Looking over at Bing's office, she saw he was facing away, on the phone, staring out at his view of the skyline. She handed Madison a file, wordlessly. Madison simply nodded and said, "Whatever's here, I'll respect your confidence and faith in me."

She took the file folder and, without looking back and acting as if anything was wrong, retreated to the executive elevators and went to her floor and office.

Once there, she told her assistant she wanted to see Troy. She had expected a raised eyebrow or two over the Rubi Cho picture; however, she guessed that her long-standing reputation as the company's biggest workaholic preceded her. No one seemed to believe the trip was anything but business. Madison didn't know if that made her feel better—or worse. Had she forgotten how to have fun all these years? There had to be a happy medium between Kiki Davis tossing her thong to the crowd—and Madison.

Troy came into her office carrying two tablets of legal paper and several pens, looking as if he was ready for a meeting.

Once they were ensconced inside, Troy shut the door and Madison tossed the file from Katherine Gould on the table.

"This came from Bing's assistant."

"What is it?"

"We're about to find out together. She was visibly upset."

Madison opened the file folder. "Holy shit!"

Inside were photocopies of some of the same pages Claire had squirreled away in her safe-deposit box. There was also what looked to be a secret memo from her father to Claire authorizing some of the shell companies.

"This looks really bad, Troy."

"Sure does."

"God, what a mess. I think Bing knows. He implied my father and I had orchestrated this whole thing. I think, as my father's handpicked choice to follow in his footsteps, Bing thinks I am in on it, too."

"I guess I'll take these pages to the forensics accountants, too."

"You know, let me hold on to them for a day or so. It's my company—and if irregular accounting is going on, I'd like to have a clear idea of what's involved."

"Okay. Watch your back."

"I'm starting to develop eyes in the back of my head from watching my back so much."

Troy left her office, and Madison glanced at her watch. It was five o'clock. No one in the office budged. Not at Pruitt & Pruitt. To succeed in the corporation, junior executives were expected to put in a minimum of sixty hours a week at the office. Most put in more, always trying to get ahead of the person at the desk next to them. Usually at seven, some people started to put on coats. At nine, a few souls still toiled, and at ten o'clock, fewer still—but the office wasn't empty. By the next day, people would start coming in around five-thirty in the morning.

Madison picked up the phone and buzzed her assistant.

"I'm going to put in a long night. Please order me up a two-liter of Diet Coke, a Cobb salad and a basket of bread rolls from the executive dining room."

Madison hung up the phone and took off her suit jacket. She rolled up the sleeves of her blouse and went over to her conference table. It was going to be a long night.

Hours later, her salad was barely touched. A croissant was half eaten and all the Diet Coke was gone. Around midnight, Madison called for the car service. She wasn't tired—and it wasn't a caffeine buzz. What Madison had discovered was so chilling that she was pretty sure she'd lie wide awake until morning.

Chapter 18

Madison burned the candle at both ends. She was developing a theory—one so bizarre she refused to share it with Troy. She barely could acknowledge it in her own mind. She pored over records and combed the Internet researching the Russian mob, in particular the Kremlin Killers, as well as going to the New York Public Library to take out several books on the Pruitt-family kidnapping.

In between all that, she had her new agenda as CEO. She had a press conference on Tuesday morning, and she was fielding more phone calls than ever.

Ryan Greene sent her an enormous flower arrangement as a token of "congratulations" on her new position, though his note was sweet enough to comment that he wished the appointment was under less stressful circumstances.

She called to thank him.

"It was nothing."

"Ten orchids and sprays of lilies of the valley, flown in from Hawaii at this time of year, aren't nothing. So just accept my thanks. Though I'm sure you're buttering me up so you can fight me over property I want in the Meatpacking district—the old beef plant I hear we both want. I'm going to put up a hotel."

"You wound me, dear Madison. Can't one friend send another friend flowers without it meaning I'm trying to gain the upper hand?"

"Not when it's you, dear, sweet, conniving Ryan." She knew he was capable of utter ruthlessness. More than one Pruitt & Pruitt employee had come to her firm after being fired by Ryan Greene, usually for reasons so preposterous Madison would laugh.

"You flatter me. Hey…in all seriousness, congratulations, but if you need someone to talk to, I'm here for you."

"Thanks."

"You going to Ellie Richardson's thing on Thursday?"

"Yes." The Senator Richardson fund-raiser, with a Christmas theme, would be the kickoff of the holiday season's whirl of social activities.

"Want to go together?"

"Can't. I have a date."

"You?"

"Am I that hard up?"

"You're stunning, darling, it's just I can't recall your last date during the social season."

"Well, I have one."

"Who is it? Julian Knight from Keller and Knight?"

"No."

"Keith Swanson—the guy running the gallery?"

"He'd be more likely to ask you out."

"He's gay?"

"Yeah. You must have no gaydar, my friend."

"All right. No more guessing. Just fess up."

"You don't know him."

"Hmm. You're being very mysterious. You know you're making me jealous."

"I doubt it. But I'll see you Thursday."

"See you Thursday. And you can be sure I'll try to steal you away from your date."

"I'd like to see you try."

* * *

Thursday lunch, Madison met her father at the intimate restaurant Chez Bella. He was waiting when she arrived, and she bent down to kiss his cheek as she reached his table.

"Hi, Dad."

"Hi." He motioned to the chair opposite and then waved a waiter over.

"Yes, Mr. Pruitt?"

"Madison, what will you have?"

"A Perrier with a twist."

The waiter nodded and discreetly disappeared.

"Dad?" Madison said as she settled in her chair.

"Hmm?"

"Dad, did your family ever talk about your brother's kidnapping?"

"Well, that's an odd lunch topic. Why would you bring that up? It's ancient history. Before I was even born, honey."

"I don't know. I was just thinking about it. Such a weird chapter in the family history."

"Well, we didn't really talk about it. Bing was the oldest, and I doubt he remembers much either—other than he once said he remembered being assigned bodyguards. Off-duty cops. But, your grandmother had a nervous breakdown, and it was just understood that it wasn't something to talk about. At least not in front of her."

"The man who did it…he always said he was innocent."

"Yeah." Her father nodded. "He was a Russian immigrant. He swore his confession was both coerced and without the benefit of an interpreter."

"Was it?"

"I don't know. I mean, there was overwhelming evidence against him, Madison. The ransom money. Baby William's clothes buried in his backyard."

She nodded. Looking at her father closely, she didn't detect any nervousness. But, like her, he was used to staring down enemies across the negotiating table. Never let 'em see you sweat was his mantra.

"Okay. I was just curious."

"Now I have a question for you."

"What?"

"Do you have any plans to introduce me to your boyfriend?"

Madison flushed for a minute. "How would you know about that?"

"My tailor, dear. You women have your hairstylists, we have our tailors."

"Damn," she muttered. "Who knew there was a tailor code of honor?"

"More like a fatherly one. Morris has a daughter around your age."

"Great," Madison said unenthusiastically.

"Well? Who is he?"

"Let's drop it. You won't approve."

"Why not?"

"For one thing, he's poor."

"So? I've met enough rich assholes for one lifetime. It takes more than money to impress me. What does he do?"

"There's the other thing. He's a teacher, not a captain of industry."

"So what do *you* like about him?"

"I can't believe we're having an honest conversation here."

"Well, if Claire's death taught me anything, it's that life is short. So what do you like about him, Madison?"

"It's hard to put into words. He's honest and principled. He's more concerned with making a difference than just…things. You know, money. Whatever. He didn't let his upbringing—poverty, gangs, all of it—define him. He's different, Dad."

"Gangs?" Her father arched an eyebrow. "Well, I'll form my own opinion. Maybe the three of us could have dinner sometime."

"Um…sure. I figured you'd be against the relationship because of the difference in our backgrounds."

"I have a little more integrity than that, Madison. Give me a little more credit. And give me a chance."

"I'm sorry. His name is John Hernandez. And when I'm with him, the whole world seems very far away."

Jack's eyes grew moist.

"What, Dad?"

"Eh…Madison, I never had that—except with Claire—and that was marred by knowing I had hurt you. Your mother and I…we never should have married. You know that. We were like oil and water. And I regret that we dragged you through the divorce of the century. I guess I thought, because you're such a workaholic like your old man, that we'd ruined you as far as love was concerned. I guess I'm just gratified that love found you anyway."

Madison reached across the table and squeezed his hand. "I guess it did."

If Madison thought the sight of John in her bed drove her mad, the sight of him in a tuxedo left her breathless.

"Well?" He cocked an eyebrow at her as he stood in her doorway.

"Oh, my God, you're so handsome, John."

He smiled and stepped into the foyer, sweeping her into his arms and kissing her. "And you look stunning."

"This old thing?" she joked, stepping away from him and twirling around in her Dolce & Gabbana. A rich emerald color, she bought the dress because she knew she would stand out in the sea of black—and it matched her eyes. It clung to every curve, and the back dipped down to the small of her spine, revealing her creamy complexion, smooth and perfect.

"Can we skip this thing and just stay home?" John asked.

"Afraid not. It would be in very bad form."

"All right then, I guess our carriage awaits us, fair lady."

He presented the crook of his arm, and she linked arms with him, feeling light, despite the confusion swirling around in her life. Madison realized what she'd told her father was true. When she was around John, she forgot the rest of the world.

Downstairs, Charlie waited with the limousine. He gave her a mischievous look, a playful wink that said he approved of her handsome date.

"John Hernandez, this is Charlie, my protector and driver and all-around friend."

John shook hands with Charlie. "Nice to meet you."

"Nice to meet you. It's good to see Madison out at this hour, instead of me driving to the office to pick her up from a fourteen-hour day. Not to mention she usually has a briefcase full of papers anyway."

Madison and John climbed into the limousine. Charlie slid behind the wheel, and soon they were easing out into traffic and heading to the Waldorf-Astoria. The ballroom had been reserved for the senator's fund-raiser. A long line of limousines snaked along the street, waiting to discharge the glittering and glamorous guests. Paparazzi had staked out a spot to snap pictures as everyone who was anyone in Manhattan disembarked on the sidewalk. However, they were hoping for a shot of Kiki or someone willing to play into their search for sex and scandal. Madison was starting to be old news, a fact she was grateful for.

When Madison and John finally arrived at the entrance, they stepped out of the limousine and entered the venerable hotel and New York institution.

Around Thanksgiving, most of the hotels, the Fifth Avenue stores and the city as a whole started ringing in the holiday season. An infectious holiday mood arrived along with the Muzak of "Chestnuts

Roasting on an Open Fire." The city embraced the holiday season with everything from wreaths suspended from light poles and hotel awnings, to holiday displays in every storefront window.

The Waldorf was no exception. A tall tree rose two stories high in the lobby, decorated with Victorian-themed Christmas ornaments. It shined and gleamed, with an assortment of colorful wrapped presents beneath it.

A smaller tree—also Victorian themed—had an entire feather motif, and was festooned with decorations mimicking ones from Victorian times made from ornate bird feathers, from peacocks to egrets.

"Wow," John whispered. "I usually have a Charlie Brown tree from the lot down the street."

"You're one up on me. I never have a tree. Too busy at work to even enjoy it, let alone remember to water it. Last year, I worked Christmas Day."

"Not this year, angel. We're spending it together."

Madison smiled at the thought. John smiled, too.

"See, the decorations make you feel like a kid again, don't they?" Madison said.

"Not really. When I was a kid, we didn't have anything like this. Ever. But it does get you into the spirit of things."

They made their way to the ballroom. It was arrayed before them like a postcard. The centerpieces on each table were miniature evergreen topiaries decorated in silver Christmas ornaments. Silver and gold festooned the room. The chairs were draped with white silk cloth and tied with gold sashes. Crystal goblets glistened under the immense chandelier, and the band was playing background music—a Cole Porter song.

Couples mingled in the area reserved for cocktails. Men in tuxedos and women in their finest clutched flutes of champagne and martini and wine glasses.

John clutched her hand at the sight of the vice president's wife, Anne Kelly, a fiery redhead with green eyes, who was charmingly outspoken and had enlivened the Washington, D.C., social scene. She waved to Madison.

"You know her?" he whispered.

"Anne? Yeah. She and Vice President Kelly own an apartment on the twelfth floor of my building. Lovely. They have a cute Jack Russell terrier named Barney. I sometimes walk him in the park—borrow him on Saturdays when I feel like I need a little fresh air."

"Man, do I feel out of place. Anne Kelly. I wish she'd run for president. I feel like…everyone knows

I don't belong. Bet I'm the only guy here with a tattoo covering his entire upper biceps."

Madison turned to face him. "Bet you're the only guy here with biceps that look sexy enough to *have* that tattoo." She lowered her voice and whispered in his ear, "I also bet *no one* else is as good in bed as you are…or has the kind soul you have. So screw them all and let's have a good time, then go home and make love all night long." She leaned back to look him in the eye, winked at him and hoped he would relax. She was rewarded with a grin.

"Anything for you, angel. I aim to please."

"And you do, darling. You do.… Well, time to meet and greet," Madison said. They approached the receiving line, and waited patiently to say hello to Senator Richardson, who was solo this evening. Her husband, a departmental political-science chair from Colombia University, was keynoting at a United Nations function. Senator Richardson was dressed in a black ball gown with a sweeping train. She was older, with honey-blonde hair tinged with frosted highlights, but her figure was still petite and trim.

"Madison, dear," Ellie greeted her.

"Hello, Senator.… I'd like you to meet John Hernandez."

"John, a pleasure."

John extended a hand.

"Are you from the Palm Beach Hernandez family?"

"No." He grinned sardonically. "I'm from the Spanish Harlem and Bronx Hernandez family."

The senator, a consummate politician, didn't bat an eye or miss a beat. "Good…I carried those districts in the election, you know."

John nodded. "I was one of the people who voted for you.… But I won't again unless education funding goes up." He winked at her, and she laughed.

"Madison, seems I have a constituent to appease."

"Yes, ma'am. And he's a tough customer. A teacher at the Harlem Charter School for Excellence."

"I've heard of it. We'll have to talk, John. And I'll have to do my best to see school funding isn't shortchanged by the Washington bureaucrats. And Madison, please give your father my regards."

"Of course."

Madison and John moved away from the senator, passing her security detail, who all had on earpieces.

"Look," John squeezed Madison's hand, "there's CeCe Goldberg and Cara Phillips."

CeCe was a major anchor/producer for a network newsmagazine. Cara was another on-air talent, a blonde with a penchant for sleeping her way to the top—at least that was the rumor Ash and the Gotham Roses had whispered on to Maddie.

"Let's avoid CeCe, if you don't mind. Her show is planning on doing a segment on Claire's murder. I really don't need her pumping me for quotes. She's a bit of a shark."

"Too late."

CeCe was charging straight at them, her perfectly coiffed brown hair not even moving a strand. Sixty, she was dressed in a dignified Oscar de la Renta red gown—befitting the start of the holiday season—and plenty of diamonds.

"Think she has enough bling-bling?" John whispered just as she reached them and stuck out her hand.

"Madison Taylor-Pruitt…congratulations on the CEO announcement. You're a mover and a shaker, that's for sure."

"Thank you, CeCe."

"So tell me, how is your father holding up?"

"Holding up?"

"I hear a grand jury may be convened as early as next week."

"My father isn't the sort to worry about maybes and innuendo, CeCe. He's far too busy for that. And you can quote me on that."

Madison smiled, but made sure her eyes were cold and unfriendly. She took John's hand and moved along without saying goodbye.

"Man…"

"What?"

"Now I know why you run that company of yours—you're not somebody to mess with. I sure hope you never look at *me* the way you looked at CeCe Goldberg."

"That old battle-ax? CeCe thrives on scandal, and on making people cry on camera. You learn really fast not to give people like that an opening."

"And I thought the mean streets were tough."

Madison stood on tiptoe and pecked him on the cheek. "We are from two different worlds of toughness. I'm glad I have you to be…myself with. We don't have to be tough with each other."

The two of them continued to "work the room," as Madison called it. They even greeted Jane Kimball, the second-in-command at the CIA. Madison knew her from a Democratic Party fund-raiser she'd attended over the summer. Jane was utterly brilliant, and one of a new wave of CIA who was fluent in Arabic—and Swahili. She was an army brat who'd lived all over the world. Madison felt a special kinship with the woman now that she herself was an agent working for the United States government. Of course, Kimball didn't know that…or did she? Madison mused.

Madison also saw several acquaintances from the Gotham Roses. They were all assigned to Renee's table. Before John and Madison could make their way there for the first course, though, Madison saw, with dread, that Fluffy Peters was making her way toward them.

"Oh, no…"

"What?"

"See this woman heading straight toward us?"

"The older woman in the tiara?"

"Yeah."

"Isn't a tiara a bit much?"

"Not for Fluffy."

"That's a cat's name."

"It's also the name of the most vicious Palm Beach socialite of them all. She winters down there, but unfortunately doesn't leave until December 10 every year, just so she can make the first round of Christmas balls in New York. Brace yourself."

Fluffy, her skin so stretched from plastic surgery that no emotion registered on her face, thrust out her hand.

"Madison, *dah*ling," she said, accentuating her syllables in an affected form of speech.

"Fluffy." Madison smiled.

"You look smashing, dear. Simply smashing."

"Thank you, Fluffy."

"And who is your gentleman friend?"

"May I introduce John Hernandez." Madison patted his arm in a gesture of affection.

"*Ohhhhh,* how lovely. Of the Palm Beach Hernandezes? I know them quite well."

"No, ma'am."

"Well, then where? Where would I know you from? The Puerto Rican sugar family? I met some of them last winter at the Breakers in West Palm. We were both there for a wedding."

"No. I'm actually from New York."

"New York? There are no Hernandezes in the social registry from New York that I know of."

"He's not in the social registry, Fluffy dear… Do tell, who designed your dress?"

Fluffy looked down, as if she couldn't remember what gown she had worn. "Oh…this? Carolina Herrera…I'm always loyal to Carolina. Now, go back. Where do you know each other from?"

"He's a schoolteacher, Fluffy. I met him through my work with the Gotham Roses."

"Oh…" She managed a wan smile, though not a single crease appeared on her Botoxed brow. "I see…I misunderstood that he was associated with your charity. I thought he was your date."

Madison decided she had had quite enough of Fluffy Peters.

"He *is,* darling. Why, we're *ever* so serious. In fact, my father can't wait to meet him. And if I could tell you the way this man drives me wild in bed… but, really, we must be getting to our table."

Madison linked her elbow through John's arm and giggled as they walked through the crowded ball-room.

"You are really naughty, Madison. Why would you do that to that poor old woman?"

"That pompous old snob? She deserved it. You can't ever use the word *poor* associated with Fluffy. Trust me."

Madison expertly steered them to their table—set for twelve—all Gotham Roses and their dates—including Ashley, accompanied by a male-model friend of hers she knew from *Chic.*

Madison sat next to Ashley and introduced her to John. Ashley introduced her date, who went by the one-name moniker Tryce.

"Nice to meet you, John." Ashley smiled as handshakes were exchanged. She was wearing a Richard Tyler gown in a rich chocolate brown, and her hair was set in pin curls, like an old-fashioned flapper.

"Your hair looks great, Ash," Madison offered.

"You like it?"

Madison nodded. "It's so different. Bet you anything you're copied, and at the next function a half-dozen women do their hair like yours." It wouldn't be the first time Ashley set off a chain reaction with her sense of style.

Their waiter came over and Madison placed her drink order—champagne. While John was ordering his drink—a cold Heineken—Ashley whispered in Madison's ear, "Forget what I said about slumming it. He's delicious. Positively edible."

Soon, their table was full, and Renee had joined them. Madison was amazed at how she greeted those at her table, not revealing in the slightest that she was anything more than the woman behind a charitable organization—certainly not a woman with a veritable mini-Quantico beneath her town home. She smiled at Madison warmly, not a single look or even a blink letting on that they were up to their necks in a dangerous case, or that Madison and Troy had nearly met their end in the Caymans.

Renee's "date" was her daughter, Haley. A pretty,

blond high-schooler, she often accompanied her
mother since Preston was sent to prison. Renee had
once expressed to Madison that she worried for her
daughter and wanted to be there for her in her father's absence. That included never scheduling more
than two evenings out in the same week. During the
busy social season, that was difficult, but Renee's
savvy solution was to take Haley along and introduce her to the cream of society, letting Haley meet
dignitaries and politicians. Consequently, Haley was
as poised as any adult in the room.

The evening progressed happily. At one point,
though, when Madison went to the ladies room,
Princess Chloe St. John—another Rose, and an
agent—accompanied her. When they were out in the
hallway, Chloe, her thick blond hair in an updo, and
wearing a stunning Richard Tyler off-the-shoulder
amber silk chiffon gown, took her by the elbow.

"Madison? Just wondering…any sign that the
Duke may be involved in your case?"

Madison shook her head. "I don't think so. This
seems personal in some way."

"Trust me, though, it wouldn't be unlike him to
make things personal if he thinks you're close to
Renee. Promise you'll be careful."

Madison nodded and the two of them went to

powder their noses, appearing to all others like two former debs all grown up. They made their way back to the table, Madison still marveling at how seamlessly agents pretended as if they were nothing more than heiresses.

After dinner, Senator Richardson gave a speech outlining her plans for social security legislation, the environment, and highway initiatives, as well as a sweeping pronouncement about free speech and patriotism that sounded remarkably like a presidential stump speech. Ashley noted that the senator's voice was firm and passionate, and she was wearing a black vintage Valentino gown as fashionable as anything on any of the twenty-somethings. She was completely telegenic. Dessert—a beautiful white cake with an apricot and custard filling and edible flowers on the top—was served, and dancing began.

John asked Madison to dance to a slow song. On the dance floor, he whispered in her ear, "I've been a very good boy, but I really want to tear that dress off you. Can we go soon?"

"Mmm," Madison murmured. "You have been a good boy. I can't believe I was worried about how you would deal with all this nonsense. You're an old pro. You sure you're not one of the Palm Beach Hernandezes?"

He laughed out loud and twirled her around.

"I'm the envy of every guy here."

"No…I think the ladies at our table are quite taken with *you*. They'll be asking you to fix them up with your friends if you don't watch it."

"Sure…and you know, I could just see Fluffy Peters on the back of a Harley."

At that thought, Madison laughed. Then Ryan Greene came up to the two of them as the song ended.

"Hi, Madison…you going to introduce me to your mystery date?"

"Ryan, this is John Hernandez. *Not* of the Palm Beach Hernandezes."

John laughed at their inside joke, and he shook hands with Ryan. Madison asked, "Where's your date?"

"Knowing Charlotte West, I'd guess she's in the bathroom checking her lipstick for the five-hundredth time this evening."

"Sounds like Charlotte."

The band started playing a song by Anita Baker, and a woman whose voice uncannily resembled Baker's was singing.

"Mind if I dance with your date?" Ryan asked John.

"It's up to her," John teased.

Madison nodded and kissed John on the cheek as Ryan took her hand and led her into the middle of the dance floor.

"Seems like a nice guy."

"He is."

"Doesn't look like one of us."

"Why do you say that?"

"The small diamond stud in his left ear. Hair a little too long. Cut of the tuxedo…too buff for Wall Street."

"God, you're observant."

"Just where you're concerned."

"Why?"

"Come on…you can have your fling with stud boy over there, but after a while, what are you going to talk about? With me, God, we can talk deals and mergers and acquisitions and all the things that make the hearts of people like us really race."

He dipped her ever so slightly and looked her in the eye. Then they resumed their dance.

Madison smiled ruefully. "You know, Ryan, there was a time I would have thought you were right. And I don't think I'll ever lose my killer instinct in the boardroom. But I realize there's more to me than mergers and acquisitions and land deals. And for some reason, he's the guy who makes my heart race."

"You and I, we're destiny, Maddie. Trust me." He winked at her. They continued dancing. Madison knew he saw *her* as an acquisition and merger he couldn't have. But that was better than *really* hurting him. He was a friend.

When their song ended, she went and sought out John, who was being "chatted up" by CeCe. He was tight-lipped and looked relieved when Maddie came to get him.

"Come on, John, let's call it a night. Excuse us, CeCe."

The two of them left the ballroom, and he said, "Man...she was determined to make me crack."

"Good thing you're such a tough guy."

"I don't know. I felt like I was being grilled by a police interrogator."

They emerged from the Waldorf, and Madison shivered slightly. She had on a light silk wrap, but the temperature had dipped to nearly freezing. John instantly took off his tuxedo jacket and wrapped it around her. Then they saw Charlie up the street and waved. He was leaning against the car reading the paper. He nodded at them, climbed back in and drove to the curb right in front of them. He hopped out to get the door for Madison as John reached for the handle at the same time.

"Sorry," John said. "Still not used to that."

"No problem," Charlie said, and gave him a clap on the back.

Madison was relieved when the heat came on in the limo right away. She shivered and shook off the cold.

"How was your night?" Charlie asked.

"Wonderful." Madison beamed. She snuggled up against John and they drove toward Central Park. "Of course, the usual social nonsense. CeCe Goldberg was after scoop, and Ryan Greene was determined yet again to create the ultimate real-estate merger, but all in all, I had a wonderful time."

"What'd you think, John?"

"I got to dance with my angel, here, so it was all good."

Madison laid her head against his arm.

"Oh, damn," she said suddenly.

"What?" John asked.

"Nothing…Charlie?"

"Hmm?" He looked back in the rearview mirror.

"Can you stop at the grocery store over on Eightieth? I just realized I forgot to ask Estelle to pick some coffee up when she came to clean today. And I cannot start my day without it."

"No problem."

A few lights later, Charlie make a left and drove

to the grocery store, parking the limo across the street from it to avoid a no-loading zone.

"Why don't you let me run in?" he asked. "Coffee...need anything else?"

"No, Charlie, it's okay...John and I will go. Maybe we'll get some fruit for the morning, too."

John opened the door for her and she slid out, still wearing his tuxedo jacket. The two of them held hands as they crossed the street and entered the supermarket.

"I took tomorrow off," John said. "I have some papers to grade, but other than that, I'm all yours."

"Great." She smiled. They took a little red plastic basket and wandered the brightly lit aisles of the gourmet grocer, filling the basket with French-roast coffee, some pastries, oranges, grapes, and some cheese and crackers.

At the register, John took out two twenties and paid for their purchases, then the two of them left the supermarket.

Suddenly, a huge explosion rocked the entire block. Madison fell backward into a pile of newspapers delivered for the morning, and John hit the sidewalk, smashing his elbow.

Debris rained down, ash and dust, and an acrid smell of burnt flesh filled the air.

With tears in her eyes, Madison looked across the street. Where her beloved limo driver had been parked with her limousine now stood the flaming wreckage of a car.

Chapter 19

Thinking fast, Madison grabbed John's hand. "Let's go!"

"What? We've got to wait for the police," he said, his voice raspy with the smoke around them.

"Trust me," she begged and pulled him around the block and then down the street to a subway station. In the distance, they heard sirens.

"Are you crazy, Madison? Someone wanted you dead. We've got to talk to the police."

Teeth chattering from shock, Madison knew she had to think clearly. She shook her head from side to side, fighting tears, trying to breathe deeply and collect herself, squeezing her eyes shut to try to stave off the vision of the burning car that she was certain was now forever etched in her mind.

"John…we've got to get to your place. Fast." She pulled him down the steep staircase into the suffocating air of the subway station. The smell of urine and stale, unmoving grimy air assaulted their nostrils.

"Give me a few dollars," she urged him. Taking the bills he handed her, she bought a Metrocard and led him through the turnstiles.

Maddie kept looking over her shoulder, moving farther down the platform. A few minutes later, she could hear a subway car in the distance, its lights a glow down the tunnel. Finally, a subway car rattled to a stop, and its doors opened with a swooshing sound.

"Come on," she urged.

Shaking his head, he nonetheless followed her. "You're in shock, Maddie. We need to go back. We're witnesses."

They hopped on the subway car. Its doors whooshed shut, and it pulled out of the station and into the dark of the tunnels.

"Where is this car headed?" she whispered.

"Not sure."

"Let's ride it for a couple of stops, get off and hail a cab to your place."

"Madison..."

"Shh..." She squeezed his hand, teeth still chattering.

Three stops later, they found themselves within thirty blocks of John's town house. They hailed a cab and were dropped off. Madison looked at her watch. It was just before midnight.

They let themselves into John's apartment, but she stopped him before he turned on the lights.

"Wait! They could be watching us."

"Who's they? Madison...what is going on?"

"You have to trust me. I need to call the FBI. Remember that man I was seen with in the Rubi Cho column?"

He nodded. "How could I not remember? I was so jealous."

"He's an FBI agent."

She conveniently left out that she was under-cover, too.

Using her cell phone, she dialed Troy, gave him her location and told him she was safe.

"Whoever did this thinks I'm dead, Troy, and that's a good thing. I need you to do one more thing before you come here."

"What?"

"I need you to use your FBI credentials to get into my office. In the upper-left drawer of the credenza against the far windows is a locked briefcase. I need you to bring it."

"Okay. Hang in there."

"Trying to."

"I won't be able to get there for a little while. I'll need to gather together a team. Give me a couple hours."

"Won't matter. Not like I'm going to get any sleep anyway."

She hung up and then John came behind her in the dark.

"Let's get out of these clothes and take a hot shower. I want to get the smell of smoke and street off of me."

She nodded and allowed him to lead her into the bathroom. They took off their evening clothes. Compared to her apartment, John's little bathroom was cramped, and the two of them barely fit in the shower stall, wedged together, their bodies close.

He turned on the hot water, still without the lights on, and pulled her to his chest. As the water enveloped them, followed by the steam, Maddie finally allowed herself to absorb—even partially—what had just happened. Great wracking sobs escaped from her mouth and she put both of her arms around John's neck, clinging to him the way a drowning person clings to a life preserver. What if he had been killed? At the thought of the explosion, she felt a pain in her heart.

Charlie was like family to her. He had guarded her with his life…had paid the ultimate price for being part of her world. Guilt consumed her, and she laid her head against John's chest and allowed the water to cascade over her, washing away some of the pain as he just held her.

After the hot water began to run lukewarm, John turned off the shower and helped her from the stall, wrapping her in a big well-worn towel. He led her into the bedroom and dug through his drawers— still in the dark, his room only illuminated by a single night-light—until he found a pair of sweatpants for her and a big sweatshirt. He donned the same— sweats and a T-shirt, then a zippered sweatshirt he sometimes wore for his morning run.

"Want a cup of tea, angel?"

Madison still had the sniffles from her crying jag. "Kind of, yeah."

She followed him into the kitchen as he readied a kettle of boiling water, his profile illuminated in the moonlight coming in through the kitchen window. Then he poured her a cup of peppermint tea and made himself one.

"I keep this tea for when I have a cold. Drink it down…. Come on, let's go to the couch."

Madison sat down. He went to get the comforter from his bed and wrapped it around her, then sat down next to her. For a long while, he didn't say anything, just pulled her against him and stroked her damp hair. Finally, he cleared his throat.

"I need to ask… Why are you involved with the FBI, Madison?"

She knew Troy would never reveal her status as an undercover operative. So she told John pretty much the rest of the story, leaving out her own involvement—Claire's death, her father, rumors of offshore accounts and the mob.

"Basically, Claire was onto something. I really can't be one hundred percent sure of what, but I have a really good theory I've been developing all week."

"So you think whoever's behind this was who ran us off the road—or tried to—at West Point."

Madison nodded, feeling almost robotic, numb.

"Can't the FBI and police protect you?"

"Yes, but until all the pieces to this puzzle are

solved and the people responsible are arrested, I can only be but so safe."

John rubbed his eyes with weariness, worry. "I don't like this at all."

"Neither do I…and every time I think about Charlie, I want to just curl into a fetal position and cry. But I'd rather get mad. I'd rather get these bastards once and for all."

In the dark, she couldn't see John's face. She curled against him and he stroked her face.

"I love you, Madison," he whispered almost inaudibly.

Madison had never really said the words to a lover. She had never even thought them about anyone else. She was too busy. Her BlackBerry was jammed full, her voice mail always overloaded, her e-mail overflowing. Love would have just been another inconvenience to fit into her schedule—right there wedged between a meeting with the board of directors and dinner with the head of the zoning commission. But this felt right.

"I love you, too."

Around three in the morning, she and John were dozing, when there was a knock on the door. John startled awake, stood and went to his peephole.

"It's that guy…from the FBI," he whispered.

Madison rubbed her eyes. "Let him in." Her body ached, and she felt as if she'd been sucker punched in the gut.

Troy nodded at John, shook his hand and identified himself, and entered with another agent he introduced as Mark Layton.

"I brought the briefcase, Madison, but before we go over all that, we want to get you to a safe house. Right now, we were able to talk to the M.E. He's saying two people were blown up in the limo—you and Charlie. That way we can keep you safe—no one's looking for you—until this is all straightened out."

"How long will that be?"

"I hope not long at all. But I can't make you any promises. All I do know is at this point, someone is very, very determined to see you very, very dead."

"What about John?"

"He's a material witness. We can hide him, too, but I think sticking a detail on him for a few days will be enough. We'll say he saw nothing. Honestly, with you dead, they probably think they're home free."

"Can you catch whoever did this? Charlie was… he was a really good man."

"We're working on it, Madison. We'll get them.

How quickly depends on what's in this briefcase you had me bring."

"Okay. So when would I go to this safe house?"

"Now, Madison. There isn't a lot of time to second-guess this whole thing."

Madison's gut twisted some more. She had gone from the height of being in love, dancing at the Waldorf, to death, grief, and now life on the run, all in the space of one night.

She turned to face John. "I have to go with them. I can't let anyone else die because of me. They'll watch you for a few days. But promise me you'll be careful."

"Forget about me, Madison. You're the one who's in danger. How can I get in touch with you?"

Madison looked at Troy.

"You can't. Not directly." He took out his wallet and handed John a card. "You can call my cell and relay messages. And I can relay them to you. But until this blows over, your best bet is just to act the role of the grieving boyfriend."

Madison rushed over to John and kissed him on the lips. "I'm going to get these guys. I'll see you soon."

Looking every bit the part of the grieving boyfriend, John nodded. "Love you."

"Love you, too."

Then, with an equally grieving heart, Madison nodded at Troy and left John's apartment, not quite sure of when—or if—she would see him again.

Chapter 20

The safe house turned out to be a nondescript motel in southern New Jersey. When they arrived at the room, Madison crashed for an hour or two on the very lumpy mattress, exhaustion overtaking her. When she awoke, Troy and two other agents—Layton and an agent named Lawson—were there, eating from a platter of cold cuts and catching some of the news coverage of her "death" on CNN.

Stock in Pruitt & Pruitt plummeted with this latest twist, but the board quickly announced the succession of Madison's uncle Bing, and Wall Street analysts thought there was the possibility of a rebound based on rumors of an acquisition of a cereal and sports-drink company.

"Frankly, Jim," one analyst said, staring at the camera, "Pruitt & Pruitt has a long history stemming from early in the last century. They invest wisely, diversify intelligently, and have had good leadership. I think they can rebound from this."

Madison padded into the bathroom and rubbed cold water on her face. In her mind, she could picture Charlie offering to go into the store for them. Then the car being blown to bits. Her only consolation was he hadn't suffered—and it was very, very small consolation.

Madison squeezed her eyes shut. When she opened them again, she sighed, rinsed her face again, then opened the toothbrush and toothpaste the agents had picked up for her—along with a hairbrush and mouthwash. She guessed they'd also go shop for some clothes for her. Though she doubted she'd be dressed in Ralph Lauren. More like whatever was on sale at the local department store. She brushed her teeth and ran the brush through her hair, then resolutely left the bathroom, ready to lay out her suspicions for the FBI.

"Guys…I'm ready to go over my theory now."

"Great," Troy said.

The motel room was shabby, and included a kitchenette with an ugly, brown Formica table and four uncomfortable chairs. Commandeering the table, Madison opened the briefcase and asked the agents to each take a seat.

"Okay, gentlemen, see if you can follow all this…. Many years ago, my uncle, the infant William Charles Pruitt III, was kidnapped and murdered. He was the second child of my paternal grandparents. My father hadn't been born yet. The case created a frenzy. Even the president of the United States at the time called the local police, as well as the head of the FBI, asking them to put all their manpower into solving the crime. It looked like an inside job. Eventually, suspicion pointed to Victor Karaspov, a Russian immigrant employed by the household as a caretaker."

Madison pulled out old photos and a couple of books from the library on the kidnapping. She had paper clips marking pages of photos. Most were in black and white.

"Victor claimed a lot of things. First, that he had no interpreter, so he didn't understand the charges. Then that he was framed."

"Aren't they all?" Lawson, a solidly built agent

with black hair and an olive complexion, said, rolling his eyes.

"I thought so, too," Madison said. "But there's more than meets the eye. Eventually, he changed his story, saying that he *had* kidnapped the baby—but not murdered him—by then the body had turned up, burned beyond recognition. He said he had a child, and he could never do anything so cruel, that he was the fall guy for a larger group of men. Later, they said a botched rescue attempt—a police raid—may have hastened the murder."

"Was he framed?"

"Well, no one believed him. But in his interviews he came across as anything but a criminal mastermind. Eventually, Victor died in prison, still professing his innocence. That's where the story ended, except for some enterprising journalists. One of them, a man named Harrison, was originally from the town where the body was discovered. He had grown up fascinated by the case and did his own investigation. He found evidence that Victor's family received a payoff—no one knows from whom. They took the money, moved away, and changed their name. Victor spent the rest of his years in prison with no visitors from his family. But his wife remarried eventually, and his daughter was apparently quite well provided for."

"Okay, so how does this intersect with you?" Troy asked. "Other than the attack at the cemetery in Venetian Lake and a false social-security number for a long-dead baby."

"Ask me the last name of the man Mrs. Karaspov married."

"I'll bite."

"Gould."

"Is that supposed to mean something to me?" Mark Layton asked.

"Christ..." Troy said, "that's the name of Bing Pruitt's assistant. Katherine Gould."

"You got it.... And there's more. Okay...so the reason—aside from the incident at Venetian Lake— that I looked at this, was that the papers Katherine gave me don't match the ones I got from Claire's safe-deposit box."

"What do you mean...don't match? They're both cooked books."

"Yeah. But *Claire's* cooked books all point to Bing approving the payments to the nonexistent William Pruitt. His signature is on a lot of the papers. And Katherine's cooked books all point to my father."

"I don't get it," Troy said, leaning over as Madison spread out both sets of false papers.

"Well, let's say Claire was on the up-and-up. She was a whistle-blower who wanted to figure out what was going on. And it would have killed her inside— if she really did love my father—to think he'd approved the false social-security number, the bogus companies, and so on. But bottom line, she would have come forward, because she was an attorney and she was moral, and that was just Claire. But someone killed her before she could meet with the FBI. *Her* books say Bing was behind the bogus companies, the mastermind. So who would want her dead? Bing. And if my father was setting her up, it's not like she would have these fictitious books out of thin air—thus, if she already had papers and ledgers proving it was Bing, then my father could let her blow the whistle, and he gets the girl, and his brother out of the way, and his company's illegal millions keep rolling."

"So the fact that the papers she had pointed to Bing leads you to believe they're the legit fakes— and Bing wanted her out of the way."

"Right. And if I hadn't gotten this other set of fakes from Katherine, I would have let it go from there. But since she doesn't know what I have from Claire, I think Katherine wants to mislead me, intentionally, and send me gunning for my own father who, on the face of things, I am angry with for having an affair with my best friend. Unbeknownst to her, he and I reconciled at a dinner this week."

Troy opened one of the library books. There was a picture of Victor's wife and daughter leaving the courthouse.

"So what did you find out about Katherine?"

"Well, according to the writer of the book, her mother married another Russian and moved to a Russian enclave in working-class Brooklyn. This became a key area for the infiltration of the Russian mob after the fall of Communism and glasnost."

"What do your personnel records indicate?"

"Her background is impeccable. She has a great education, and she clearly has elevated herself above where she came from. I see her in the office. She dresses beautifully, carries herself like an aristocrat."

One of the agents stood and went to the small refrigerator and got a bottled water. "So how do you know it's not a coincidence? Gould isn't all that unusual a name."

"I thought about that, too. So I went digging further. It's her mother, all right, who was married to Victor. Then I did some discreet asking around on the office grapevine. Turns out, I never knew, but when she first joined the company years before, she worked for my father."

"Your father? How come you didn't know that? You work there, too."

"Yes. But this was long before I was working at the company, around the time of my parents' divorce. I was eleven or twelve. Office scuttlebutt has it that Katherine and my father had an affair. My mother found out about it…the affair was one of a thousand indiscretions on my father's part. So it wasn't like anyone put much stock or credence into it. It was never common knowledge. But the timing of the whole affair was unfortunate. Even if it was just rumor, my father didn't need to give my mother's lawyers ammunition. Right around that time, Katherine suddenly goes to work for Bing."

"So who's idea was the whole scheme to set up the offshore accounts, to have William on the books, the whole nine yards?" Troy asked.

"Well, I think Katherine carried the torch for my father for years. Call it woman's intuition. If she and Bing began an affair, I think she introduced him to the Russian connection…and I'm not sure why he took the bait, but he bit all right."

"So how do we catch the bastard? And her?" Troy asked.

"He thinks I'm dead. What if I show up to a private meeting with him? Confront him. Shock him with the fact that I'm not dead. I wear a wire. I get him to fess up. You cowboys sweep in, you get the bad guys, I get my old life back. We're all happy. Case closed."

"I don't know if I like that," Troy said. "Too many variables. Bing is volatile. Gould has connections to the mob. I don't like it. I really don't. Preliminary look at the limo points to C4. Fucking C4 explosives. These people don't play around, Madison."

"And neither do I. Treat me like an agent, Troy. Not a friend. I don't think you'd hesitate to send one of your female FBI agents into harm's way. And I am not staying in this sorry motel for the rest of my life. I already miss my Egyptian-cotton sheets."

Troy finally cracked a smile.

"Great… This is what I get for working with heiresses."

Chapter 21

The night before Madison was due to confront Bing, she couldn't sleep.

In the first place, she was emotionally exhausted by the relentless coverage of her death. And she was tormented by guilt at seeing her father—and Ashley, and even her mother, who normally could drive her insane just by being on the same continent—all torn to pieces by the funeral. The FBI told her that they couldn't risk placing the people she loved in jeopardy by revealing she was alive. Their grief had to look real—the better for the confrontation with

Bing. They even provided her father and mother with ashes, which were buried in the family plot in Rye, New York. Bing served as a pallbearer, which infuriated Madison. She had never been particularly close to him. After all, the Pruitts were known for their stoicism. It wasn't like she'd grown up with warm, fuzzy memories of him.

Then there was lower-key, but still in the papers, coverage of Charlie's funeral, attended by old pals from Vietnam, as well as her father and other people from Pruitt & Pruitt who had gotten to know Charlie over the years.

Madison tossed and turned restlessly. She missed John. She missed talking to him. She missed sleeping next to him. She wanted to go back to the life she was trying to create.

Finally, she gave up and went out to the kitchenette where Troy was already drinking coffee.

"What's your excuse?" she asked.

"Hmm?" he mumbled sleepily. "My excuse for what?"

"For not sleeping. What's up with you?"

"You know, working side by side with you these last couple of weeks…it's hard to then separate the friendship and know I'm going to put you in a vest and surround you with snipers and hope this guy doesn't go off the deep end and try to kill you. They've nearly run you off the road, shot at you, blown up your car…"

"Next thing you know, they'd have put cyanide in my martinis." She tried to make him smile, but Troy was grim-faced.

"I ever tell you I lost my first partner?"

"No," she whispered. She pulled up a chair.

"Yup. A woman. Great person. Had just found out she was pregnant, too, and was going to ask for a transfer to a desk job. Husband was an awesome guy, completely gaga in love with her. A secret-service agent. They met in D.C. We were all on assignment there. I was an usher in their wedding party."

"How'd she get killed?"

"We were undercover on a case involving money laundering. Not unlike this one. Drug kingpin, in that case. He somehow got wise to her—she was acting as one of his kids' nannies. She traveled with him and his family. He had two wives of all things. Some kind of sick fucker. Anyway, he killed her—shot her stone cold in the center of her forehead—right in front of his eleven-year-old son. Told the kid he had to be able to do things like that if he wanted one day to be the kingpin himself."

"Oh, my God…" Maddie whispered. She patted Troy's hand.

"I…she didn't see it coming. None of us did. I was grateful it happened in a split second, but I took a leave of absence for a month. Really had to think about whether I could handle this job."

"I'm glad you didn't quit. We might never have met."

"Yeah…but it never gets easier. Not really. You toughen up. You learn to tell yourself it's all part of the risks. That we're all working for the greater good. That it's the eternal battle of good versus evil, white hats versus black hats. That we're on the side of the righteous. But if you care about people, you never get used to watching them go out there in a vest."

"You know, going through all this…it makes me *more* determined to be an agent. I'm really proud that Renee asked me to join."

"Even if you always have to hide that side of your life from John?"

She nodded. "I told him no more secrets. But I guess I tell myself this is different. Like you said, it's for a greater cause. But I'm also good at it. I was the one who put the puzzle together. I can do this, Troy. Renee's faith in me wasn't misplaced. She was right. I can make a difference in a way I never thought possible."

"All right then, Agent Pruitt...go wash up and get ready. Today's the day."

"We're going to get him, Troy."

"Let's hope you're right."

Madison rose and turned to go to the bathroom. Two agents were posted outside the motel room.

"Maddie?"

"Hmm?" She turned her head to look at Troy.

"Do me a favor? Wear this?" He took a silver chain from around his neck, a ball design like the kind for dog tags. Suspended at the bottom was a medal.

"What's this?"

"It's Saint Christopher. It was my partner's. I guess I'm superstitious. I want you to wear it."

"Then I will," Madison said. "Thank you, Troy."

Maddie turned from him, her eyes wet with tears. She'd be damned if she was going to let Troy lose another partner.

Chapter 22

The plan was to surprise Bing—and Katherine.

Bing was scheduled to speak at the ribbon-cutting ceremony for the waterfront tower property. Katherine—Troy found out by hacking into her scheduler at work—was going to accompany him. Troy had managed to plant a bug on the lapel of Katherine's suit jacket, which she had left that morning on the back of her desk chair for a few minutes, so the FBI was listening in on their conversations in the limousine.

After the ribbon-cutting, Bing and Katherine

were driving to look at a piece of property farther south. It was a fairly open space, also waterfront, and snipers would be posted on the tops of the four warehouses surrounding the area. Once Bing and Katherine got out of the limo, ostensibly to meet the Realtor who'd told them she would be arriving in a Mercedes, Madison would exit the car instead.

In the Mercedes would also be three agents, all crouching. On the way to the meeting site, Madison tested and retested her own wire. She tried to breathe normally, despite the weight of the vest and the way it constricted her rib cage. And she told herself over and over again they were going to get them.

In the vacant lot, the minutes ticked by. Madison saw two vans full of agents, but they were battered old vans that would never arouse suspicion. She reminded herself they were full of men and women ready to protect her at all costs.

Troy reassured her, "Look…he's expecting a Realtor, not you. Most especially not you. You're armed, you're wearing a vest. We've got you covered from every angle. The bottom line is, we're looking for something to hang him and Katherine with— rather than risking that they somehow twist this and pin the whole scheme on your father, or worse, cover their tracks so well they hire a Dream Team defense and get away with it. So we're looking for a confession of sorts."

"What if they see you guys?"

"We've done this a hundred times before, Madison. Again, they're not expecting this. *You* see that van. *You* see the guys on the roof. They see an abandoned warehouse area and a piece of property they want to buy. They see the Mercedes of the Realtor they're meeting."

Madison inhaled and exhaled a few times. Troy's cell phone rang.

"Yeah...? Okay. We're ready."

He hung up. "They're five minutes away." He spoke into his wristband, which had a walkie-talkie built into it. "Five minutes, people. Remember, Madison is going to be in the thick of things. At all costs, she is to be protected. Hold fire unless I give the signal. No one get trigger-happy. Let's do this. And let's get them."

Five minutes later, Bing and Katherine's long, black limo pulled into the gravel area in the center of the four old warehouse buildings. Their driver parked and leaned his seat back, expecting to wait for the two of them as they toured the land. Madison saw him take out a newspaper and start reading.

Bing and Katherine climbed out from the back of

the limo, shut the car door, and were talking. Katherine pointed through the warehouses—you could glimpse the Hudson River through the buildings. Madison knew how their minds worked. They loved the property. Hell, if she wasn't on the case, she'd buy it herself.

Madison waited until their backs were turned slightly, and then she climbed from the Mercedes after a whispered "Good luck" from Troy. Almost involuntarily, she fingered the medal around her neck.

"Hello, Bing. Katherine…" she said as she stood and they faced the direction of her voice.

"Oh, my God," Katherine said.

Bing's face was drained completely of color. "How…? How…?"

Madison shut the door of the Mercedes and took a couple of tentative steps toward them.

"Surprised to see me?"

Neither one of them said a word.

"Yeah…shocking, isn't it? I just refuse to die. You blew up my limo driver, but miraculously I didn't get blown to smithereens. I'm still standing."

Bing glared at Katherine. "I thought you said you'd take care of everything."

"I did."

"Well, someone screwed up. It's obviously not

taken care of if we still have the former acting CEO of Pruitt & Pruitt standing right in front of us."

"Sorry to disappoint." Madison stared at them coolly. "Katherine…why?" Madison asked. "I've sung your praises at work…thought you were absolutely someone who was essential to our organization. Why? I mean, not only did you frame my father, but you were willing to kill me…and Claire?"

"I *was* Claire," she said, her voice tinged with bitterness. "Years ago. I was the girl who fell in love with Jack Pruitt, who believed in him. Believed in his high ideals. And then he discarded me. Worse, he passed me off to his brother. Like I was something to be traded."

"So why didn't you move on, Katherine? Why didn't you leave the company, find another job?"

"Pruitt & Pruitt was my life."

"You mean your obsession. Does Bing know?"

"Does Bing know what?" Bing snapped.

"He doesn't, does he?" Madison suddenly felt more confident. This wasn't unlike a boardroom meeting, setting the scene, making a case. Manipulating the players if need be.

"I don't know what?" Bing's face registered annoyance. Madison knew he hated being in the dark about anything—surprises were his least favorite thing in the world. They once gave him a surprise fiftieth birthday party—and at the Plaza, no less—and he didn't speak to Jack or Madison for a month afterward.

"Nothing. It's nothing." Katherine waved her hand in the air dismissively. "Ignore her."

"Oh, no…it's something, all right. Why don't *you* tell him, Katherine? You tell him."

"Tell me what? What is she talking about? This is madness. Get to the point."

"Do you know Katherine's real name?"

"Of course I do. Katherine Gould."

"No, no, no, Uncle Bing…" Madison was mocking him, inciting his fury further. "The name on her birth certificate. The name she was *born* with. The name she had when she went to the courthouse. To watch her father's trial. Poor little immigrant girl with her kerchief on. Thick accent. Ugly black shoes. Hand-me-downs. Tell him, Katherine. Tell him all about it. Or should I say Katarina?"

Katherine Gould stared with pure hatred at Madison. "Shut up, you pathetic bitch. You spoiled, spoiled, worthless girl."

"Guess it'll be up to me to clue in poor stupid Bing. That's why you're not CEO—or won't be for long. Too gullible. Don't have the temperament needed to have a position of that power."

"Shut up!" Katherine shrieked. "Just shut up, now!"

"Her real name, Uncle Bing, is Katarina Karaspov."

Bing didn't react—not at first. It took a second for the name to seep into his brain. Madison watched it, almost as if watching a movie in slow motion. Then she finally saw the recognition dawn on him.

He turned to Katherine. "What? You're…the… the daughter of that beast who killed my baby brother?"

"My father didn't kill anyone. He was railroaded by the system. By a system that couldn't see past his thick tongue, his accent, his ugly black shoes, like she just said. A system set up to revere people like the Pruitts and despise people like the Karaspovs. Immigrants. Use us like workhorses, then turn on us in an instant."

"But he killed my brother. He…burned him."

"He didn't. He wasn't capable of it. He turned that child over to the men he worked for. It was supposed to be a clean job. They were supposed to give him to a nursemaid—to his own former nanny to care for him. Hell, she loved him more than his own stupid mother. She was too busy with her bridge club to even tuck her children in at night."

Bing's face was pale, and he had broken out in a sweat. "I can't breathe," he said, clutching at his throat.

"My father took the fall for his partners in crime, in return for enough money for me to go to college, for my mother to buy a house. But I knew he was innocent. And though I was the little immigrant girl, I made sure I got straight A's, that I worked two jobs, that I had the 'right clothes,' the right look, the right hairstyle. And I spent years—long relentless years—researching the Pruitts. I know more about the lot of you than you know about yourselves."

"So you went for the job with my father with malice aforethought."

"Absolutely. And along the way, he fell in love with me. And I became enamored of him. I changed my plan from ruining the Pruitts to the ultimate irony—becoming their matriarch. Marrying into them in the ultimate realization of the American dream."

Madison looked at Katherine's face. She was flushed, heady with the dream she'd once embraced.

"Then he threw me out like I was worthless. Or worse, old. I saw him going for younger women.

Women who weren't even fit to converse with him, let alone share his bed. Then that Claire…for God's sake, she was *your* age. That was too much to take."

"But what about me?" Bing asked, horrified. "What about me, us. Our dream?"

"You're so stupid. Really…do you think you hold a candle to me? You've never been bright enough to compete with your brother—or me, for that matter."

"But we were going to run Pruitt & Pruitt together."

"You're a fool. A stupid old fool," Katherine said. "Men really never outgrow thinking with their pants, Madison. They're not like women. Not like us."

Madison realized Katherine had said more than enough for the FBI, but she needed to know if Bing was a pathetic patsy or a full participant, especially where the murders were concerned.

"Bing…okay, I get that maybe you were jealous of my father—had a sense of brotherly competition, but…why go along with her plan? You have enough wealth for a lifetime and then some. Why? I don't understand."

"I was so tired of the attention he got, Madison. Him and his *golden-girl offspring,* while me, I had two ex-wives and no children." His voice was laced with a nasty sarcasm. "Katherine's too old now. I guess I…she came to me with a plan. To increase my wealth tenfold through working with money that we could hide offshore. No one would know. And at the same time, we were creating a set of books that would topple your father's reign as CEO. I'd never heard a more perfect plan in my entire life. It was sheer brilliance."

"Bing—" Madison shook her head sadly "—my father loves you. You're his only brother. He feels protective toward you."

"Please…don't patronize me," he snapped. "Once he came along, he was all my mother cared about. He got the attention, he got the love, and I was shunted aside, this ugly reminder of William's death. Then my father chose *him* as the heir to the throne of Pruitt & Pruitt. He chose *him* to lead the family into the new century. Me? I was an afterthought."

"Bing, you run a huge part of the company. You've been on the cover of *Fortune* and been profiled in the *Wall Street Journal*. You're delusional."

"Would a delusional person have so perfect a plan? And it would have worked…"

"Except for Claire."

"Except for Claire. So we had to get rid of her."

"Bing," Madison shook her head. "But kill her? How?"

"Katherine and I figured out she was snooping around. So it was a preemptive strike. I told Claire that I knew Jack was crooked, and I had proof. If she met me at the warehouse, I would give her the evidence. Once she got there, friends of Katherine's erased her. End of story."

Madison was stunned. Claire had gone there knowing the evidence might point to Jack. But she was willing to hunt for the truth, just as Madison was. Her admiration for her friend's courage grew.

"And me? Getting rid of me?"

"If your father had married Claire, as was his plan, they would have had babies, and you, my dear, would have found your fortune divided many more ways—maybe even eradicated entirely. But once Claire was gone, I realized that if Katherine could arrange for your demise, too, then Jack would be completely and utterly destroyed. Only putting him in prison for illegal accounting practices would be the cherry on top."

Madison was chilled. The two of them were stark raving mad, and now she had enough evidence on both of them.

"Well, your plan failed, you two. I'm still alive."

Madison started to back up to the Mercedes, but Katherine pulled a gun from her purse.

"Sorry, my little blond heiress. Now it's your turn."

Suddenly, SWAT teams made their presence known. A male voice shouted from the rooftop, "Freeze. Put the gun down…you're surrounded."

The Mercedes's doors opened, and out stepped Troy and his team, their automatic weapons drawn and trained on Bing and Katherine. At the same moment, Bing grabbed Madison and thrust her in front of him as a shield.

"Hold on, everybody," Troy said, holding his arms up and urging calm.

Katherine trained her gun on Maddie's head—right at her temple.

"If anyone moves one step closer, she's dead."

"Now…you do that, and you're in a heap more shit, Katherine. That's a capital offense…needle-in-the-arm kind of crime…" Troy spoke calmly, in a measured voice. "We don't want this turning into a bloodbath."

Madison tried to weigh her options, and found they were rather slim at the moment. If the SWAT teams could take out Katherine, she felt she could handle Bing, but the gun butt pressed to her temple was limiting any choices she had.

"I'd rather die right here than go to prison like my

father," Katherine said. "And taking a Pruitt brat with me will only make my demise truly spectacular and worth it."

"No one's killing anyone here, Katherine," Troy said, inching his way forward.

Katherine and Bing, meanwhile, were inching their way backward with Madison.

Suddenly, Madison's heel caught in a small rut in the gravel-and-concrete lot. As she fell and lost her balance, Katherine herself fell backward for a second, which was all Troy's SWAT team needed. They shot her what seemed to Madison like a hundred times, and her body shook from the impact of dozens of bullets striking her like a target at target practice.

That left Madison and Bing, who were now wrestling on the ground.

He had his hands clasped around her throat, on top of her. Madison knew there was no way they could shoot him without risking the bullet traveling through him and hitting her. Taking her fingers, she gouged his eyeballs, and he let out a high-pitched squeal.

Rolling off her, Bing grabbed Katherine's gun, which had fallen to the ground right by them. He couldn't see, but he felt for Madison, who was rolling away from him. He grabbed her hair and brought the gun toward her. At that moment, the SWAT team had a clear shot—and took it…

Just as Madison's uncle Bing pumped two shots into her—one just below where the vest protected her…and one in her thigh.

Madison felt as if she'd been punched with fire. The world started going black, the sky turning to stars.

The last thing she saw as she turned her head was Bing, his body moving as it was riddled with bullets, and then Troy…saying, "Hang in there, Madison!"

And then…

Nothing.

Chapter 23

Madison next woke up three days later in the hospital intensive-care ward. Morphine clouded her brain and she had no recollection of anything. She felt pain, but it was softened by the morphine. She felt fear, because she saw the machines around her.

And then she saw John's face.

She relaxed a little at the sight of him. He stroked her face, and said something like, "You did it…they got them…. Don't talk…I love you."

And then blackness.

* * *

The next time Madison awoke, she felt stronger. She still didn't remember much. She could recall Charlie and the limo blowing up, and Bing…and being wired. But the precise way she got shot was a blur.

Her father was there, looking ashen, next to John. "Darling…don't speak. You're getting the best medical care money can buy."

Madison's eyes focused, and she saw three private-duty nurses around her. If she could have, she would have laughed. She couldn't move—what did she need three nurses for?

Her father said, "Bing and Katherine are dead. Claire's murder solved. I'm cleared…but at what price?"

She mouthed the words "How bad?"

"Your vital signs are stronger now. You lost a lot of blood. But you're a tough one. Of course, anyone who has seen you in action in the boardroom knows that. And you were lucky. The bullets missed major organs. And the one in your leg missed your femur."

Madison trained her eyes on John and smiled.

Her father said, "He hasn't left the hospital. He's a good man, Maddie, love…I'm very happy for you.

So now you've got to pull through and get out of this damn bed and home where you belong."

Madison grimaced as pain started coursing through her spine.

"Nurse!" her father shouted protectively. A nurse appeared with a syringe…and Madison fell backward into space into a sweet morphine oblivion.

The next person she saw was Troy.

"I sent John to a hotel to shower and get some sleep," he said. "Your father is having a press conference right now. Everything's going to be okay, Madison."

She nodded. She felt more alert. "Thanks," she whispered. "Water?"

Troy looked over at a nurse, who approached the bed with some ice chips, which she spooned into Madison's mouth. The soothing cold wetness trickled down her throat.

Troy looked at the nurses. "I need five minutes with her."

They nodded and left them alone.

"The Governess is really grateful on this one, Madison. Really grateful. If you weren't undercover, trust me, you'd have a drawerful of medals."

"Just…glad…it's…over."

"Sure. Me, too. I guess you can retire to your penthouse now."

She shook her head. "I'm going to…walk," she croaked. "Then kick your ass."

He winked at her. "We'll see, tough girl, we'll see."

Madison looked over at the windowsill. Huge flower arrangements, spectacular showy ones, stood in crystal vases.

"Ryan Greene, CeCe Goldberg—of course, she wants an exclusive, Anne Kelly…Christ, the president, Renee, Ashley. You got so many flowers, we started sending some to the cancer ward…try to brighten a few patients' lives a bit."

"Good."

Madison smiled. She was going to be fine. She knew it. And the hell with anyone if they thought this meant she was going to quit the Gotham Roses secret spy division.

Epilogue

Troy called Madison at work a couple weeks later.

"Hey…is this my old partner?"

"Oh, my God, Troy…how are you?"

"Fine. Assigned to a new case but missing my old partner. I keep bugging Renee to find us something new to work on."

"That would be great."

"How's the office?"

"Feels good to be back, even if I'm still recovering from the ordeal. But I was going crazy cooped up in the hospital and then at home. On the bright side, my father is CEO again and I'm second-in-command. Stock is healthy…we're building, climbing…doing great, Troy."

"And John?"

"Wonderful."

"You two set a date yet?"

"Sometime next summer when he has off from school. We want to marry in Tuscany."

"Some guys have all the luck."

Madison fingered the medal she still wore around her neck.

"Troy?"

"Yeah?"

"I still have your medal. I need to get it back to you."

"Nah…you keep it. I want you to have it to keep you safe."

"Thanks."

"Listen, this isn't an entirely social call. I need for you, your father and John to meet me somewhere."

"Why do you need them?"

"You'll see." He sounded mysterious. "Renee actually has a surprise for you. But I need to deliver it to keep your real relationship with Renee a secret."

"All right," she said cautiously. "Where?"

"Drake Hotel. The restaurant. Eight o'clock on

Friday. Reservations will be in my name. Table for five. Just sit and order a cocktail and wait for me. Don't be late."

"But—" she said, but found herself listening to dead air.

How odd, she thought.

On Friday, she and John and her father took her father's limousine to the Drake. As she sat in the back with them, she couldn't help smiling. "Out with my two favorite guys."

"Well, we're with our angel," John said. He wore a Hugo Boss suit she bought him for his birthday. Her father came in his suit from the office, and she wore a simple black suit by Calvin Klein with a cream-colored blouse. In her hair was an antique comb John had bought her at a street fair they went to in Greenwich Village. Filled with marcasite and emerald stones, it had tiny art deco–looking butter-flies.

They arrived at the Drake at a nudge before eight o'clock. As Troy had said, there was a table waiting for them in the back. The maître d' said, "This is the table that was requested. Very private."

Their waiter, with an elegant French accent, took their drink orders, and they sat back and looked at each other. Madison assumed they were all thinking the same thing. What the hell were they doing there, and why was this FBI agent acting so…well, downright cloak and dagger?

At eight-fifteen, Madison checked her watch. "Okay," she said aloud what was on her mind. "The suspense is killing me."

Five minutes later, the three of them—they had all sat with a view of the entrance to the restaurant—saw Troy walking in with a tall gentleman.

Troy approached the table—and he was beaming.

"Thanks for coming," he said. "I'd like to…well, the hell with dragging this out. I'd like to present to you your uncle, Madison…your uncle William Pruitt."

Madison's father nearly choked on the water he was sipping. John dropped his bread knife. And Madison felt that if she stood, her legs would fail her.

"What?" Her voice was tremulous.

The tall man—who did look remarkably like her father—leaned down and pecked her on the cheek. Then he shook John's hand, and walked to the other side of the table and stared at Madison's father.

"Jack…" he said hoarsely. "It's true."

Jack stood and embraced him, fiercely, overcome with uncharacteristic emotion. The two of them stood there for several long minutes. Then everyone sat down and Madison said, "Troy, what's going on?"

Troy and William smiled, while her father—perhaps for the first time in his life—looked understandably shaken.

"Well…while you were laid up, Madison, we went through Bing's and Katherine's apartments with fine-tooth combs. But even before that, something was…well, as the expression goes, 'sticking in my craw.' Remember how Katherine, when confronted, pretty much admitted everything?"

"Uh-huh."

"Well…one thing she wouldn't admit, didn't admit, was her father's guilt in the murder. She said he had kidnapped the baby, but the child was supposed to go to his nursemaid who loved him like a son."

"I assumed it was a woman who refused to believe her father was capable of the ultimate evil."

Troy shook his head. "I don't know. It seemed like more than that to me. So I started digging. And digging. Madison, Jack…I am telling you that I never worked so hard on anything in my life. Dead ends, false leads…but eventually, I found him. With my boss," he looked at Madison meaningfully, "pulling some strings."

Troy looked over at the man next to him.

"Are you…sure?" Jack asked hesitantly.

"Yes. Despite him being a dead ringer, we ran some DNA tests using Madison's blood from the hospital. He's your brother."

Jack covered his mouth with his hand and started weeping. "I'm sorry…this isn't like me. It's just that…"

"I know," Troy said calmly. "It's a little overwhelming. I'll let William tell you what he knows."

William cleared his throat and fiddled with his linen napkin. "I was too young to remember anything, of course. I only knew that my mother loved me dearly—my adoptive mother. My nursemaid did take me in, but whether from fear or guilt, after just a month or two, she allowed me to be adopted by a wonderful family—a college professor and his wife in Vermont. Lovely people, who had no idea who I was or where I was from. The adoption was handled privately. The nursemaid had a fake birth certificate claiming I was hers. She said she was a single mother whose parents disowned her and she felt I would be better off with two parents."

"And you had no idea?"

"None. I knew I was adopted. Mom told me when I was seven. They never had any more children, and to be honest, they doted on me so much that I didn't feel like I was overly curious. When my father passed away—I idolized him, such a wonderful man, so revered at the University of Vermont, taught history—I started thinking about it some more. My mother and I tried to find my birth mother. But some things didn't add up. The birth certificate, we discovered early on, was fake. So it seemed like we were at a dead end. I just…let it be. I assumed it was just the way it was."

"Then, when I showed up," Troy said, "it all fit together."

Madison and Jack began peppering William with questions. Was he married? Did Madison have cousins? Was his childhood happy? What did he do for a living?

Madison was delighted to discover her uncle was a professor at New York University—in the history department like his father before him. He specialized in the history of Europe in the twentieth century. He had, he said, a very happy life, other than occasionally looking at the starry sky and asking those big questions, like *who am I* and *where did I come from?*

His wife was also a professor—she taught English, and specialized in medieval literature and Chaucer. He had a daughter Madison's age who was a schoolteacher like John, and a daughter three years older than Madison who was a stay-at-home mother of a little boy.

"What do they think of all this?" Madison asked.

"They're so grateful I'm at least getting the opportunity to meet…you all."

Then he looked down, suddenly somber.

"What?" Jack asked. "We didn't scare you off with all our questions, did we?"

"No…I just…well, it's important to me that you know I'm not interested in the Pruitt fortune. Money's not important to me. I just wanted the opportunity to know where I came from. Honestly."

Madison's father waved his hands. "Look, William, after all I've been through watching Madison in that hospital bed…I'm determined that we build a relationship. I'm still stunned. Still…overwhelmed, frankly. But I'm also telling you that your daughters will want for nothing in life. Your grandson will have a trust. They can do nothing with the money, or they can donate it, or they can enjoy the good life for a while. You and your wife can continue teaching…or she can go to England and spend the rest of her life haunting medieval monasteries researching old manuscripts. The money is yours. It's your birthright. But we'll let the lawyers figure all that out. For tonight—" he raised his glass "—we celebrate."

Madison, John, Troy, William and Jack all lifted their water glasses or wineglasses and clinked.

Madison looked around the table. Pruitt-family secrets very nearly killed her.

But now...now she believed that Pruitt-family secrets just may have opened up a whole new world to her.

One she couldn't wait to start exploring. She couldn't believe the twists and turns her life had taken recently. As her father and William tried to catch up on lost years, Madison's cell phone chimed. She kissed John on the cheek and excused herself to take the call in the hotel lobby.

"Madison?"

"Renee?"

"Do you like your surprise?"

"I don't even know what to say. I can't believe it."

"The Governess pushed hard to find him. She—and I—are delighted with your hard work and this was one way to say thank you. You're an asset to the organization and we'll use your skills again, you can be sure. Until the Duke is locked away, the Roses aren't safe."

"Count me in. Only next time I could do without the gunshot wound," Madison said wryly.

"Ah, that Type A personality. Somehow, Madison, I knew you'd want to work with us again."

"Never challenge a Pruitt. We don't like to lose."

"And neither do the Roses. Take care, Madison. Go enjoy your dinner."

Madison said goodbye and closed her cell phone. Renee was New York City's keeper of secrets, and Madison was certain of one thing: the Duke—and anyone on the wrong side of the law—had better not underestimate the power of the Roses.

* * * * *

*Turn the page for an exclusive excerpt
from the next book in the exciting*
THE IT GIRLS *mini-series
from Silhouette Bombshell.*

Flawless
by Michele Hauf

*On sale September 2006
at your favourite retail outlet.*

Flawless

by

Michele Hauf

London—Scotland Yard

Green and crimson fire escaped myriad facets of
the diamond. Cut in the asscher style—a stepped
square cut with cropped corners—each slight tilt or
turn of the jeweler's tweezers released another scin-
tillating wink of color. Even beneath the harsh fluo-
rescent lights of Scotland Yard's interrogation room,
the rock put on a show.

There must be a flaw. Nothing in this world was
perfect.

At the back of her thoughts Becca Whitmore heard whistling. Symphony No. 8 in B minor? That one of the Scotland Yard inspectors would cruise down the hallway whistling Schubert made her smile. Someone must have stepped out on the town last night for a bit of culture.

"Miss Whitmore, I am told?"

Thoroughly startled by the male voice, Becca dropped the diamond. It clinked onto the Formica table and then jumped onto the creased ultrawhite card she always used to lay out gemstones.

A whistle acknowledged her jumpiness. "Sorry," the man offered. "Will dropping it damage the thing?"

Tucking her hair behind her ear, Becca resumed her composure. "No."

Why then had she been so jumpy about dropping the gem? It was too early, and she was still on New York time, which should find her snuggled in bed.

"Diamond is one of the hardest substances found in nature, Mr...."

"Agent Dane."

A slender, six-foot-tall advertisement for laid-back leaned in the doorway to the interrogation room, wearing a presumptuous smile and a pale blue turtleneck sweater. Tufted blond hair warred for one direction on his scalp, and lost. Right hand cocked at his hip flared back a black tailored suit coat to reveal sculpted pecs beneath the snug sweater. The Brits had a thing for close-to-body tailoring, as if they still clung to the 60s-era style.

Swank, Becca thought.

He tugged out a leather badge wallet from inside his coat pocket and flashed it quickly. "Agent Aston Dane. MI-6."

The wallet snapped shut as Becca stood and offered her hand. "Becca Whitmore."

Grasping her hand with both of his, he pumped twice. A simple band circled his right thumb. Silver? Cool, relaxed. Thumb? Open. She had a knack for judging a person by the jewelry they wore. Men, most particularly, offered intriguing analysis merely for the subtleties their choices uncovered.

"Nice to meet you. Could I see that badge again?"

Still holding her hand, Dane winked. "You show me yours, I'll show you mine."

Becca tugged her hand from his grip. A lift of her eyebrow challenged. "I don't need a little slice of plastic to prove my credentials."

"Oh? And yet, who the bloody hell *is* Becca Whitmore?"

"I'm the gemologist."

"Ah! Yes, the expert in gems imported from the good old US of A. I was told an American was making the trek. From the JAG?"

He referred to the FBI's Jewelry and Gem program. They only worked thefts in the United States, and so had handed the case on to the CIA. The CIA had been the one to contact Becca's superior, Renee Dalton-Sinclair.

This case had begun in New York, but had quickly gone international with today's theft in London.

Yesterday's attempted theft involved a request for a very specific ten-carat diamond—the very diamond sitting on the white card, Becca presumed. The New York gems dealer had told the thief she'd sold the stone, and then he'd shot her in the head.

The victim? One MaryEllen Sommerfield. Becca knew the woman from the occasional purchase or meeting at a gems convention. MaryEllen was still alive, a bullet lodged in her frontal lobe as if a ticking time bomb. Surprisingly, she remained coherent, and had been able to give the details to the questioning officers.

She'd also told the officers she'd sold one ten-carat stone to a London jeweler who had plans to create a necklace for a Transylvanian countess, and another to a Paris dealer. Had the thief been aware there were two stones? He hadn't made such knowledge apparent to MaryEllen.

Becca's cover was more than a story; she actually was a gemologist. But she was so much more. Recruited into the Gotham Roses four years earlier by Renee Dalton-Sinclair, Becca served as an agent in an undercover operation that concentrated on crimes committed by the rich and untouchable. Those "good ole boys" who lived above the law and could get by with nearly anything—yes, even murder— merely by flashing their cash or the incredible power of political connections.

On the surface, the Roses were made up of young socialites who focused on charity and giving back to the community. Nary a crime fighter in the bunch. Hardly the sort the criminals would expect to come beating a path in their wake.

Less than two dozen of those exceptional young women were aware of and worked for the covert branch of the Gotham Roses, which cooperated with the CIA, FBI and other crime-fighting agencies.

Fate had placed Becca in the path of a fleeing purse snatcher several years earlier. Reacting to instincts she'd never known she possessed, she'd swung her Fendi bag, catching the thief in the face and laying him out flat. Renee Dalton-Sinclair had witnessed this scene from the back seat of her limo.

Renee Dalton-Sinclair was a gorgeous and powerful woman married to Preston Sinclair, a noted businessman who had been incarcerated for embezzlement. The scandal had been the motivating force behind Renee's creating the Gotham Roses. Renee answered to a mysterious woman the Roses knew only as the Governess. Becca often wondered if she were CIA or FBI, or someone higher.

No matter, the Governess had made it clear she wanted intel on this case—and hard evidence. Suspicions from unnamed sources suggested there was something different about these two diamonds.

What had Agent Dane asked? Ah, was she with JAG.

"I'm not at liberty to discuss my orders," she finally said. The usual excuse. Scotland Yard knew the CIA had sent her here. "You said you're with MI-6?"

"We're the obvious match for this case—" His pause ended in a forced smile. He smoothed his palm down the front of his thin blue sweater. Summoning the truth or concocting a lie? It was the kind of pause Becca was familiar with, and used herself, when needed.

"So what makes you believe this case is organized crime?"

Agent Dane stepped backward and slapped a hand over the wall next to a large picture window. The expanse of glass changed from a light-blocking white to reveal it was actually a two-way window.

"Exhibit A," he offered, crossing his arms and ankles to pose beside the scene.

Inside the room sat a thin man in black sweats. Blood trickled down his stubble-darkened jaw. A vivid purple bruise marred the left side of his forehead. Hands secured behind his back, his head hung, and his shaved scalp revealed a scar that curved around his ear.

"Is that the thief?"

"You'd bloody better believe it. Picked him up as a lovely bonus prize along with the diamond. Sergei the Dog, a middle-tier thief."

"Middle-tier?"

"Sure. You've got your scummy low-class blokes who do smash-and-grabs and tilt over little old ladies on street corners." He ticked off his fingers as he explained. "You've got your upper tiers who do exquisitely planned heists. And then there's the middle, who are basically all the rest. They work in groups or are hired by the big blokes who haven't the time or motivation to delegate the upper-tier heists."

"I see."

"Good on you, Miss Whitmore. I like a woman who picks up the ball without fumbling. There's also a notation on Sergei's record that he's snitched for the SVR. Er, that's the—"

"I know what the SVR is."

"Stupid Violent Russians."

Becca compressed her lips and crossed her arms. "What is it about the Russians you don't like?"

"Besides the Cold War?" He shrugged. "It's a joke. You know, humor?" He sighed and punched a fist into his opposite palm. "Tough room. SVR, Russian intelligence," he said. "But isn't that an oxymoron? Russian. Intelligent?"

Despite her reservations, Becca had to smile at that one. Ah, hell, she let out a chuckle.

"Whew. The room is finally starting to warm up." Dane's smile was easy and it piqued Becca's attention. Yes, definitely an open man. Direct opposition to her need to keep things close. "So the CIA has flown you all the way over to London for that pretty little rock?"

Nodding and exhaling a sigh, she said, "Don't remind me of the flight."

"Don't like to fly in airplanes?"

"I fly well enough, it's over water that makes me,

mmm—" she tilted her palm up and down "—nervous."

"Hydrophobic?"

"Yes." And, far too much information to reveal to a perfect stranger.

He gestured to the diamond. "A nice piece. Ten carats, I believe. Snatched earlier this morning from a gems dealer over in Liverpool. But I don't understand why the entire store was not ransacked. There were other gems of equal size, yet this bit of sparkle was the only thing taken."

"It is curious nothing else was stolen," she agreed. "There was no sign of forced break-in at the New York store. The dealer said the thief specifically asked for this stone. As if he knew she had it. And yet, she had only purchased it five days earlier."

Picking up the diamond, she redirected her focus. Hefty. Solid. The asscher-cut was rather ugly. Herself, she preferred the classic round brilliant-cut stones.

Either way, it was an extraordinary showpiece. A stone this size would likely be utilized as the key setting in a necklace or brooch. Only the wealthiest of wealthy could touch such a fine piece, a social set with which she was familiar.

What troubled Becca was that someone had tried

to kill for this diamond. Murder didn't seem necessary. Had the London theft been foiled by the arrival of Scotland Yard? No time for murder? Or had the thief's MO changed? Was this even the same thief who had struck in New York? Or had that man alerted another in his gang to the sale?

If it was organized crime, as Agent Dane had alluded, the scenario seemed likely.

She fished out a disk light from her valise. It was a little larger than a quarter; a snappy little device Alan Burke had designed for her. A squeeze of the rubber case produced UV light on one side and white light on the other side. Alan was the gadget guru for the Gotham Roses, who operated out of the brownstone on Sixty-eighth Avenue. Alan never met a challenge he couldn't fill or a foreign movie he didn't like.

Leaning over the table to block some of the unnatural overhead light, Becca beamed the ultraviolet light across the diamond. As expected, the diamond fluoresced. But wow, it fluoresced…pink! Most diamonds fluoresced blue, and fluorescence wasn't necessarily favorable when pricing a stone. More fluorescence tended to make the diamond murky, sometimes oily in color when viewed in natural daylight. As an attribute it was prized only if the fluorescence cut the yellow in the stone to produce a blue-white color.

But this stone wasn't yellow; in fact, it was quite clear.

"That's odd." Flipping the light disk to white light, Becca then tilted the diamond to redirect the blocks of prismatic color beamed across the white card. There was something…

Startled at her discovery, Becca turned the crown of the diamond toward the tabletop. By beaming the white light through the lower pavilion of the gem, it produced a kaleidoscopic dance of light on the pale gray Formica. Within the glow, small, dark spots littered the colors…in a pattern.

Letters?

"There's something on the table of this diamond. An ion beam brand?" she spoke her suspicions out loud.

Dane leaned over the table. "There's something inside the diamond?"

"I'm not sure." Becca held up the diamond before him. "There is a method jewelers use to mark diamonds in a minute manner. It's completely invisible to the naked eye, unlike the oft-used laser engraving burned into the girdle. This is the girdle." She ran a finger around the edge of the diamond. "Ion beam branding deposits identification codes or matrices inside the diamond, which are only viewable with a high-powered microscope."

"And where is yours?"

"Not here. The 200x microscope required is too large to lug about in my little case. But what makes the discovery strange is that I didn't need it."

She flashed the light over the crown of the diamond. Just one more check. Indeed, a faint pink glowed within the stone.

"Brilliant."

"Yes, but check this out." She flashed the white light across the stone. "Hell."

"So that's where diamonds come from, is it, Miss Whitmore? Hell?"

This time, Becca did not see anything. No letters or branded matrix. In fact, the marks she had seen were now completely gone.

"This isn't right—"

"Oh, blighted bollocks!" Dane dashed from the room.

Whatever had bit him in the ass?

Becca spun to the two-way window. She jumped up and rushed to it, slapping her palms to the glass. The suspect convulsed on his chair.

Dane appeared and grabbed the man by the throat. White spittle oozed over his tightly clamped lips. The agent pounded a fist against his chest then released the bound man with a thrust. Still strapped to the chair, the man fell backward, landing on the floor, his feet in the air. He didn't move.

Dane shouted, "Sod me!"

He flung his arms out and turned to approach the two-way window. He gave the glass a good pound with his fist. Anger stretched his mouth to a tight sneer.

He kicked the chair leg, and exited the room.

Becca rushed to the open door and peeked out to find Agent Dane standing in the hallway, hands to hips and head shaking. He looked to her and fisted the air again. "Bastard killed himself."

0806/18a

SILHOUETTE®
Sensation™

PENNY SUE GOT LUCKY by Beverly Barton

The Protectors

When an eccentric millionaire leaves her riches to her beloved dog, Lucky, Penny Sue Paine is assigned as his guardian. But it seems someone wants this pooch dead. Enter Vic Noble, a gorgeous ex-CIA operative hired as Lucky's protector. Suddenly Penny Sue thinks *she's* the one who got lucky!

THE INTERPRETER by RaeAnne Thayne

Mason Keller took the unconscious woman he found in the middle of the road to recover at his ranch. Jane Withington couldn't remember why she was in Utah, but her language skills were superior…and her attraction to Mason was undeniable. As they tried to uncover her identity, could they escape the terrible threat from ruthless terrorists?

WILD FIRE by Debra Cowan

The Hot Zone

Firewoman Shelby Fox witnessed a murder and her life was plunged into danger. As she and old friend Detective Clay Jessup hunted a killer, an attraction between them which had long lain dormant burst into flames, and everything changed…

On sale from 18th August 2006

Available at WHSmith, Tesco, ASDA, Borders, Eason, Sainsbury's and most bookshops

www.silhouette.co.uk

0806/18b

SOMETHING WICKED by Evelyn Vaughn

Bombshell: The Grail Keepers

Kate Trillo cursed her sister's killer, but in doing so had cursed herself. And now it seemed that she might even have cursed the *wrong* man. Kate would have to delve into her heritage and find a long-lost goddess grail to learn the truth. But would the truth see that justice was done?

THE MAKEOVER MISSION
by Mary Buckham

When librarian Jane Richards ended up in an island kingdom with Major Lucas McConneghy, she was at a loss as to what he could want with *her*, until she saw it was her stunning similarity to the queen that had brought her there. And with danger lurking everywhere Lucas might be protecting her, but he was putting her heart at a greater risk...

FLAWLESS by Michele Hauf

Bombshell: The IT Girls

An elite jeweller had been shot, diamonds embedded with military secret codes were missing...and the Gotham Rose spy and gemologist Becca Whitmore was on the case. Blazing a trail through Europe with her partner, MI-6 agent Aston Drake, to find the stones and the shooter, could Becca stop the codes from falling into the wrong hands, before it was too late?

On sale from 18th August 2006

*Available at WHSmith, Tesco, ASDA, Borders, Eason,
Sainsbury's and most bookshops*

www.silhouette.co.uk

▼ SILHOUETTE®
INTRIGUE™

THE SHERIFF'S DAUGHTER
by Jessica Andersen

Medical investigator Logan Hart could never resist a damsel in distress. And seeing bullets fired at Samantha Blackwell brought out all of his protective instincts. But soon some chilling new evidence came to light... Was the target really Samantha, or Logan?

HER ROYAL BODYGUARD by Joyce Sullivan

Crown Prince Laurent Falkenburg was determined to protect Rory Kenilworth, even if that meant disguising himself as her guard and denying the attraction between them. Because this beautiful Californian girl was much more than a new princess threatened by assassins...she was *his* betrothed.

LAWFUL ENGAGEMENT
by Linda O Johnston
Shotgun Sallys

Cara Hamilton's reporter's instinct could smell the corruption in Mustang Valley, but she needed sexy lawman Mitchell Steele on her side to get the job done. Mitch wanted to prove his father had been murdered, and teaming up with Cara was no hardship, but would truth, justice and love prevail on judgement day?

MYSTIQUE by Charlotte Douglas
Eclipse

Trish Devlin had gone undercover at the exclusive Endless Sky resort to find the truth about her sister's disappearance. But the plot only thickens when Trish meets the enigmatic and attractive O'Neill. With more questions at every turn, can she get to the bottom of *all* of Endless Sky's mysteries?

On sale from 18th August 2006
www.silhouette.co.uk

0806/SH/LC146

SILHOUETTE BOMBSHELL

Presents

RICH, FABULOUS...AND DANGEROUSLY UNDERESTIMATED.

They're heiresses with connections, glamorous girls with the inside track. And they're going undercover to fight high-society crime in high style.

www.silhouette.co.uk

SILHOUETTE

Presents

ATHENA FORCE

CHOSEN FOR THEIR TALENT.
TRAINED TO BE THE BEST.
EXPECTED TO CHANGE THE WORLD.

*The Women of Athena Academy are back in
five new high-octane adventures.*

The story continues with these five books

www.silhouette.co.uk

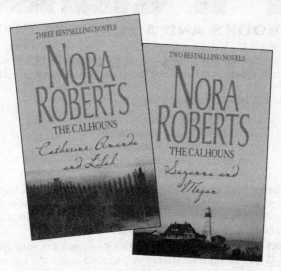

FREE

4 BOOKS AND A SURPRISE GIFT!

We would like to take this opportunity to thank you for reading this Silhouette® book by offering you the chance to take FOUR more specially selected titles from the Sensation™ series absolutely FREE! We're also making this offer to introduce you to the benefits of the Mills & Boon® Reader Service™—

- ★ **FREE home delivery**
- ★ **FREE gifts and competitions**
- ★ **FREE monthly Newsletter**
- ★ **Books available before they're in the shops**
- ★ **Exclusive Reader Service offers**

Accepting these FREE books and gift places you under no obligation to buy; you may cancel at any time, even after receiving your free shipment. Simply complete your details below and return the entire page to the address below. You don't even need a stamp!

YES! Please send me 4 free Sensation books and a surprise gift. I understand that unless you hear from me, I will receive 6 superb new titles every month for just £3.10 each, postage and packing free. I am under no obligation to purchase any books and may cancel my subscription at any time. The free books and gift will be mine to keep in any case.

S6ZEE

Ms/Mrs/Miss/Mr...................................Initials ....

BLOCK CAPITALS PLEASE

Surname ....

Address ....

....

....Postcode ....

Send this whole page to:
The Reader Service, FREEPOST CN81, Croydon, CR9 3WZ